P9-CLB-386

Unhappy Returns

Elizabeth Lemarchand

Unhappy Returns

WALKER AND COMPANY
NEW YORK

First published in the United States of America
in 1978 by the Walker Publishing Company, Inc.

ISBN: 0-8027-5375-2

Library of Congress Catalog Card Number: 77-80205

Printed in the United States of America

10 9 8 7 6 5 4 3 2 1

All places and characters in this story are
entirely the product of the author's imagination.

To
Béatrix Mead

Chief Characters

ERIC LACY	Archdeacon of Marchester
ROBERT HOYLE	Rector of the amalgamated bene-fices of Pyrford and Amber-combe
GEORGE ALDRIDGE	proprietor of the Pyrford Stores
MATTHEW GILLARD	owner of Ambercombe Barton, a large prosperous farm
MARGARET GILLARD	his wife
ROSEMARY GILLARD	their teenage daughter
HUGH REDSHAW	A successful writer, living at the Old Rectory, Pyrford
ETHEL RIDD, of 2 Quarry Cottages, Ambercombe	housekeeper to the late vicar, Barnabas Viney
BILL SANDFORD, of 3 Quarry Cottages, Ambercombe	history tutor at the Westbridge College of Education
DETECTIVE-INSPECTOR HARRY FROST	of the Whiteshire CID
DETECTIVE-SUPERINTENDENT TOM POLLARD	of New Scotland Yard
DETECTIVE-INSPECTOR TOYE	of New Scotland Yard

PYRFORD

A prosperous village on the main road skirting the western edge of the Whitehallow Hills. Attractive cottages of the local honey-coloured stone. An interesting church (St Michael), mainly fifteenth century, but retaining a good fourteenth-century tower.

AMBERCOMBE

A tiny parish of a few farms and cottages in the White-hallow Hills, a mile north-east of Pyrford, originally a manor of Tadenham Abbey (q.v.). The small twelfth-century church (St John the Baptist) was built by the monks for their tenant farmers and has several Norman features.

From Wanderings in Whiteshire
by H. R. Cawthorne, FSA

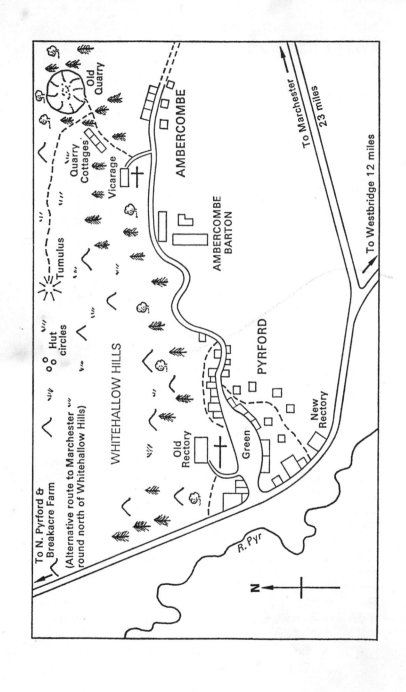

Prologue

The door-bell rang. Eric Lacy, Archdeacon of Marchester, grimaced, hastily signed a letter and tossed it into a wire basket on his desk. He sat reorientating his thoughts as sounds of the caller's admittance reached him. A few moments later a cleric in early middle age with a sensible pleasant face was shown in.

'Come along in, Hoyle,' he said, getting to his feet with hand outstretched. 'Glad to see you. Still more glad that you're accepting the living. Come and sit down. My wife's bringing us some tea presently.'

The archidiaconal study was an attractive room, low-ceilinged and book-lined with windows overlooking the Cathedral Close. A blustering December afternoon was sending scats of rain against them, but inside it was warm and cosy. Robert Hoyle looked around appreciatively. Well up to Plumstead Episcopi standards, he thought. Except, of course, that Mrs Grantly wouldn't be bringing in the tea herself . . .

'Well,' the Archdeacon said, when they were settled in a couple of armchairs, 'Pyrford-with-Ambercombe won't be exactly a bed of roses, but what living is these days? But I'm convinced you're the right chap for the job, Hoyle. You're country bred, with just the right sort of experience, and a good age to make the move. Forty-five, isn't it?'

'Near enough. Next week, actually.' A slight frown furrowed Robert Hoyle's brow. 'I only hope you're right, though, about my being the chap for the job, Mr Archdeacon. One knows how dicey these parish amalgamations can be. Not that I've heard any protests while I've been down there. I thought there seemed to be a sort of general resignation.'

'That about sums it up,' the Archdeacon agreed. 'Neither parish is keen on the idea, naturally. Pyrford aren't used to their parson having other commitments. David Massinger was doing awfully well there, and it was most unfortunate that he got an offer of higher things so soon after Barnabas Viney's death left Ambercombe vacant. Ambercombe people feel that they'll lose their identity, but of course it just isn't on for a place with under a hundred inhabitants to have an incumbent of its own these days.'

'Pyrford made it pretty clear that they're afraid of having to carry the can financially,' Robert Hoyle observed.

'George Aldridge who runs the Pyrford Stores, the new senior churchwarden, got on to it at once, I suppose? Did he weigh in right away about selling some of the Ambercombe church plate to pay for the urgent repairs to the building?'

'He did. I was completely non-committal on the subject. What are your views, Mr Archdeacon?'

'In this particular case I can't see where else the money can come from. It's going to cost a packet to put the church in order. A small community like Ambercombe can't possibly raise it, and could never repay a loan from the diocese. We've tried the Historic Churches people, but they say they can only foot a relatively small part of the bill.'

'Is the plate valuable?' Robert Hoyle asked.

Archdeacon Lacy pursed his lips and shot up his bushy eyebrows, further elongating his hatchet face.

'Not outstandingly. Rather clumsy Georgian silver. Old Viney kept it in the bank – unnecessarily, I should have thought, although there have been a couple of quite serious church robberies in the diocese over the last two years. He only had the stuff out for major festivals. There's a Victorian set for ordinary use. But I should think the Georgian plate would well cover the essential repairs, anyway.'

Robert Hoyle asked about the prospects of getting a faculty for the sale.

'Reasonably good, I'd say. Of course, there'll be some opposition from Ambercombe people. The Gillards, for instance. Quite nice sensible people, and he's the modern progressive type of farmer, but they're a bit static in other ways. His family has farmed Ambercombe for centuries. You'll have met his wife, of course: the new junior warden. And the late Barnabas Viney's housekeeper won't take to the idea kindly. I'm afraid you've got her for keeps. She's a militant holy hen, who's moved into a cottage in the village and is caretaking the vicarage until we can sell it. But whether any of 'em will go to the length of lodging an objection to the petition when it goes to the Consistory Court, I can't say.'

'The late Barnabas Viney seems to be a sort of legendary figure,' Robert Hoyle said. 'I can hardly take it in that he was at Ambercombe for *fifty-two years*. You say he had an absolute fixation about reviving monastic worship in the parish because of the church having been founded by Tadenham Abbey?'

'Fixation is the word. Hence his flat refusal even to discuss his retirement. He realised, of course, that amalgamation with Pyrford would follow, so he hung on, living in monastic style and reciting the Divine Office *in toto* every day of his life. There was really nothing we could do. At eighty-eight he had a regular Sunday service, and there was always a celebration on Saints' days. Parish organisation was virtually nil, but imagine the public furore if we'd seriously tried to winkle him out ... Well, shall we make a start by discussing possible dates for your induction?'

Chapter 1

Robert Hoyle's induction to the living of Pyrford-with-Ambercombe took place early in March. In addition to the upheaval of moving house, and making, with his wife Jean, the acquaintance of his critically interested new parishioners, he was also immediately involved in preparations for Holy Week and Easter. It was hardly surprising, therefore, that Ambercombe's problems temporarily faded from his mind, but on the Tuesday before Easter they were abruptly brought back to it by a visit from Mrs Gillard of Ambercombe Barton. On going to answer a ring at the front door soon after breakfast, he found her on the step, a brisk, rather sharp-featured woman with a fresh complexion, wearing slacks and a car coat. She had called, she told him, for the authorisation to collect the church plate from the bank as she normally did.

'Mr Viney always had it out for Christmas and Easter and the Patronal, Mr Hoyle,' she said, a hint of defensiveness in her voice, 'so people'll be looking for it Sunday. As I'm going into Westbridge to do a bit of shopping, I thought you might be glad to be saved the journey.'

'It's very kind of you to think of it, Mrs Gillard,' Robert Hoyle replied, realising that he had completely forgotten the Archdeacon's information on the subject, and narrowly missed dropping an outsize brick. 'Come in for a moment while I write the bank manager a note. Sorry my study's still in a mess.'

'Shifting must be a terrible job,' she commented, taking the chair he drew up for her, and looking around. 'I only hope it won't come my way for a long while yet. I've never had but two homes in my life: my Dad's over to Thurlstoke, and now my husband's. But Mrs Hoyle seems pleased with the New Rectory here, from what she said to me at the welcome party.'

'We both are,' Robert said as he wrote. 'We're thankful

that it's small and easy to run, without being a box, like some of the modern ones. I don't think we could have faced the Old Rectory.'

'A ramshackle great place,' Mrs Gillard agreed. 'Mind you, Mr and Mrs Redshaw have modernised it from top to bottom, and done it up lovely. All right if money's no object, of course, him being a famous writer.'

Robert decided to put out a feeler.

'Talking about doing places up,' he said, 'I understand there's been a suggestion that some of Ambercombe's church plate should be sold to raise the money for all the repairs that have got to be done. How do you feel about it, Mrs Gillard?'

Her colour came up quickly, and she made an unconscious movement of planting her feet more firmly on the floor.

'I'm dead against it, Mr Hoyle, and so's my husband. He's not much of a one for going to church, that I'll admit, but he's Ambercombe born and bred, and his family before him. They've farmed the Barton time out of mind. And we don't think it's right that what folk that's dead and gone gave to the church should be sold now. Why can't the diocese find the money, seeing what they get in from the Quota, and that we're only a handful of people out here?'

'I'm afraid that it's the usual story of too many needs chasing too little money, you know,' Robert said, addressing an envelope. 'But the decision on selling the plate doesn't rest with the parish, does it? We should have to apply for a faculty from the Consistory Court of the diocese.'

He glanced up and met her uncompromising steady gaze.

'I know about that, Mr Hoyle, being warden at Ambercombe for quite a while. And I know if you object you can write in and say so. We're not ones to make trouble, Matt and me, and we don't want to stir any up for you, seeing you've barely set foot in the place, but it's only honest to say that if it comes to going to court, we'll have to speak up.'

He held out the letter that he had just written and smiled at her.

'Thank you for being so frank, Mrs Gillard. I'm glad to know what you think. Of course I've had no time to go into things yet.'

They walked down the path to the rectory gate discussing the arrangements for Easter services at Ambercombe, and he sensed that she was mollified. A girl of about fifteen was sitting listlessly in the passenger seat of the estate car outside.

'That's your daughter, isn't it?' Robert asked. 'I remember her at the party.'

'That's right, Mr Hoyle. She's on holiday now, of course. Rosemary, here's the Rector.'

Quite a pretty child, he thought, as he tried rather unsuccessfully to get her to talk to him. Rather pale and withdrawn, though. Mum a bit overwhelming, perhaps?

'Looks a bit peaky, doesn't she?' Mrs Gillard remarked, echoing his thoughts and slamming the car door vigorously. 'Girls always outgrow their strength at her age. Well, thank you, Mr Hoyle, and I'll be dropping in the plate box round dinner time, if that suits.'

The car drove off, and he went back into the house. Jean Hoyle, small and cheerful with dark curly hair and bright brown eyes, was organising the contents of her kitchen cupboards. She broke off and perched on a windowsill to be briefed by her husband on Mrs Gillard's visit.

'I suppose it's a foregone conclusion that the PCC will vote for selling the plate,' she said when he had finished. 'And it doesn't sound as though the Gillards have any other ideas about raising the money, does it?'

'No. I think there's very little doubt that the faculty would be granted. But it's all so unfortunate. I mean, the last thing you want is a divisive brawl when two parishes have just been amalgamated. I wonder if it's really necessary to have as much done to the building as the diocesan architect chap says in his report? I've got to go up to Ambercombe now to fix up Easter communions for a couple of bedridden old birds, and I think I'll have a detailed look round on my own. Back about twelve-thirty, when Mrs Gillard's due to drop in the plate.'

Over the centuries Pyrford had grown in the shape of a T, the crosspiece along the main road to the west of the White-hallow Hills, and the stem running up a small valley to

15

Ambercombe. At the intersection was the village green, with the church on the north side and the Old Rectory on rising ground behind it. Facing the church on the opposite side of the green was the pub, the Seven Stars, and the Village Stores. The New Rectory, as it was still called locally, post-war and purpose-built, was on the main road, a short distance to the south. Robert Hoyle emerged carefully in his elderly Austin 1100, and turned right. A second right turn brought him to the Village Stores. He parked and got out to buy some stamps, but paused briefly for the pleasure of looking about him.

In the clear sunlight of this bright March morning Pyrford looked enchanting. Colour was intensified. Against the honey-gold of the cottages, flowering trees, daffodils, climbing japonica and clustering purple aubretia made a brilliant mosaic. A green flecked tide was rising on the wooded lower slopes of the Whitehallows. Higher still, the sun touched the outcrops of bare rock, bringing them to life in a still dead land of winter-bleached grass and rotted bracken. Over it all in the soft blue vault of the spring sky larks were singing. Round and round the War Memorial a small boy pedalled a red tricycle in total absorption.

Robert Hoyle shook off the recurring sense of incredulity that his lot could have fallen in such a place, and plunged resolutely into the Village Stores. Early days though it was, he knew instinctively that he would never be *en rapport* with George Aldridge, the proprietor, and his wife. Mabel Aldridge, a pale bespectacled woman with straw-coloured hair, could never meet your eyes, and confined her conversation to a variation on the theme of your last remark. Her husband, also pale, with sharp black eyes and a small black waxed moustache, was unstoppably voluble. As senior churchwarden of the now combined parishes and a keen business man, he was never at a loss for a topic needing immediate discussion where his rector was concerned. The sight of Robert Hoyle at the post office counter brought him hurrying across from the bacon slicer.

'Morning, Rector. *And* a proper spring morning this time. It's a bit of luck you've chanced to look in. A young chap was in here yesterday about a new oil distributing

16

company starting up in Westbridge. Sureglow's the name, and they're offering churches a special discount on fuel oil. Here's their price list, if you'd care to take a look, and I've written what we're paying now alongside. We'd stand to save a nice little bit from the look of it. I've been over to check up on the tank, and –'

'It's certainly worth looking into,' Robert cut in. 'Of course, we'd have to weigh up any cash saving against losing the goodwill of our present suppliers. I understand they've always been very satisfactory.'

'You're right there, Rector. Dead right,' George Aldridge agreed, with the camaraderie of one keen business man talking to another. 'That'll be one thing more to go into after Easter.' He shot a keen look at Robert Hoyle. 'We shan't be looking for a job then, and that's a fact ... Have they been on at you up there about getting the Ambercombe plate out of the bank for Easter? Plain ridiculous, I call it, seeing the size of the congregation they get.'

'Mrs Gillard is kindly fetching it for me this morning,' Robert replied, and was unable to refrain from adding that he was on his way up to Ambercombe to arrange about Easter communions for the bedridden. He hurried off, raising a hand in greeting and suppressing a grin, aware of the disapproval radiated by George Aldridge and two Pyrford housewives who had just come into the shop.

Two minutes later he was driving up the winding road to Ambercombe, which ran through coppices bursting into leaf, and between hedges starry with celandines and primroses. It gained height steadily, and finally swung right past the well-kept farmhouse and buildings of the Barton. Fifty yards further on there was a pull-in by the church gate where he parked, setting off on foot to pay his parochial calls.

Half an hour later, having made these, he returned to the church, a small sturdy building with a diminutive belfry. Before going inside he circumnavigated it, scrutinising the roof. This was in worse condition than he had realised, the crumbling stone tiles encrusted with moss and lichen, the guttering broken in several places, and ineffective-looking patching having already been carried out. A completely new roof was obviously a must. A couple of thousand quid at least at current prices, he thought. Being so off the map was bound to run up costs.

He paused briefly by Barnabas Viney's grave close to the south wall. A granite cross bore the inscription 'BARNABAS VINEY 1886–1974. Rector of this Parish 1922–1974. Faithful Unto Death. Seven times a day will I praise Thee, O Lord.' The grass had been neatly clipped, and there was a bowl of primroses. Robert Hoyle wondered who had paid for the cross. The redoubtable Ethel Ridd, perhaps, who so far had declined to recognise his own existence beyond attending services held in the church.

There was a tiny south porch, and a door of oak, black with age, set in a Norman arch with rough zigzag mouldings. It stood open, a screen of wire netting protecting the interior from birds and stray animals. Robert unhooked it and stepped into the dank chilliness, blinking to adapt his eyes to comparative dimness. There was a small fifteenth-century east window, but the others were Norman lancets, deeply splayed in the massive walls. There were damp patches on the latter, and the plaster was crumbling in several places. Catching sight of traces of powdered wood on the uneven stone floor he glanced up anxiously at the roof timbers. The diocesan architect was urging renewal of these, and of the bell supports: the two medieval bells had been silent for years. And of course it would be hopeless to do all this unless some proper heating could be put in, he thought, contemplating an elderly Aladdin stove.

His eye was caught by movement. The young green of trees was visible through the plain glass of the east window, and their swaying branches formed a living reredos for the altar. The deficiencies around him seemed suddenly to fade into another and more significant picture with a quality of timelessness. Almost primitive in its simplicity, this church had borne witness to the faith and skills of its founders through seven centuries. Successive generations had altered it but little. A few enrichments had been added: a Jacobean oak pulpit and font cover, and one or two memorials, but miraculously no devastating Victorian restoration had taken place. Robert Hoyle knew at that moment that his mind was made up. If there was no other way of raising money for the preservation of this treasure entrusted to his care, the Georgian plate must go. His resolution was confirmed by the sight of a framed list of the vicars of Ambercombe in attractive lettering, spanning the centuries back to one HENRICUS *c.* 1180.

Suddenly remembering that he was also nominally responsible for the vicarage until it was sold, he left the church and crossed the eastern end of the churchyard to the gate leading into its garden. As he expected, the latter was rapidly reverting to nature. The vicarage itself, a pleasant if dilapidated two-storey building, was raised on a low terrace, and to his surprise all its windows were wide open. As he stood staring at it he remembered that Ethel Ridd was caretaking. Then there were approaching footsteps, and a man of about his own age, hirsute and in jeans and sweater, came round the side of the building.

'Blimey!' he exclaimed. 'Our new man of God, I presume?'

Robert Hoyle saw, and liked, a humorous face with lively blue eyes and a wide mobile mouth.

'One of my new parishioners, I take it?' he queried.

'Geographically, yes. Ecclesiastically, I'm a write-off, though. Bill Sandford. God, padre, you gave me a turn! I thought for a moment it was old Barny. He haunts the place, you know. I saw him distinctly the other night. Admittedly I was on my way home from the Seven Stars.'

Robert Hoyle grinned as the new arrival came down a short flight of steps and joined him.

'Did you know him well?'

'Probably better than anybody else in the place. The fact that we'd both succeeded in doing our thing was a sort of bond, I suppose. The old chap honestly thought his life's work was reviving monastic worship here. He was perfectly happy tootling backwards and forwards to that morgue of a church to say matins and lauds and whatever. I used to drop in for chats, and do things for him in Westbridge after they wouldn't renew his driving licence. He wasn't in the least senile, you know. Just a bit fragile towards the end. How are you getting on with the Ridd?'

'At the moment I'm completely unacceptable, I'm afraid,' Robert Hoyle replied, declining a cigarette.

'A god-awful woman,' Bill Sandford said with feeling, cupping the flame of his lighter in his hands. 'She's just not true! Six foot if she's an inch, and wears a knitted cap with a great bobble on the top. Booms like a bittern. Doesn't it put you off when you're officiating?'

'It is a bit disconcerting. I suppose she was devoted to Barnabas Viney?'

'Utterly. Saw herself as a sort of acolyte to a holy man. The hell of it is that she's landed next door to me. I've got one of the workman's cottages up by the old quarry. I needn't say I'm *persona non grata*, like you. I cut through here instead of going round by the road just to get her goat – she's supposed to be caretaking at the vicarage until it's sold. Airs it, and so on.'

Bill Sandford indicated the open windows.

'What's your own thing?' Robert Hoyle asked, harking back to an earlier stage in the conversation.

'Mine? Oh, I'm as near to a drop-out as I can afford to be. I used to lecture in history at a London Polytechnic until an aunt left me nearly enough to live on. I fetched up down here, and get by on part-time at the Westbridge College of Education. Living instead of existing. I'm just on my way to the Stars for a pre-lunch beer.'

'Can I give you a lift down?'

'Thanks. My bus is in dock at the Pyrford Garage at the moment.'

As they walked through the churchyard Bill Sandford alluded to the projected sale of the church plate.

'I hear there's a move to flog it,' he said on an interrogative note.

'I've no idea if the PCC will want to apply for a faculty,' Robert Hoyle replied guardedly.

'Worth a packet, isn't it?'

'I didn't get that impression from the Archdeacon. Rather average Georgian, I gathered. I haven't seen it myself.'

Bill Sandford seemed reluctant to abandon the topic.

20

'Georgian? There must have been earlier stuff at one time, surely?'

'Oh, undoubtedly. But records in a remote parish like this are pretty sketchy as a rule,' Robert Hoyle replied, getting into his car. He leant across to unlock the passenger door, and feeling that he had had enough of the Ambercombe plate for one morning, changed the subject.

Before he reached home, however, it cropped up yet again. Just after dropping Bill Sandford at the pub he saw a figure in a brown suede coat approaching, and was hailed. Recognising Hugh Redshaw of the Old Rectory, the well-known writer of breathlessly dynamic detective fiction, he stopped and let down the window. A reddish face with enquiring grey eyes and a small toothbrush moustache presented itself.

'Well met, padre! I've just dropped in on your lady wife to ask if you'd both care to come up to dinner with us next Wednesday, when the Holy Season's over? She wasn't sure if you were clear, and said you'd ring us back.'

While recognising an attempt on Jean's part to leave a loophole, Robert Hoyle decided to accept the inevitable.

'As far as I know, we are,' he said. 'Thanks very much.'

'Good man! Come along and get your strength up for the Parish AGM. I see that the explosive topic of the Ambercombe plate's on the agenda. Believe me, it'll be rich. As my appalling potboilers would say, black passions seethe under the surface calm of the village life.'

Robert Hoyle received an amused conspiratorial look which he found irritating. Controlling himself, he smiled pleasantly in return, remarked that almost everything must be grist to an author's mill, and extricated himself on the plea that his wife had laid on an early lunch. As he drove on he wondered gloomily how long it would be before he could give his undivided attention to normal parish business.

In the event, the Parish Annual General Meeting turned out a damp squib to those in hopes of an exciting firework display, although there was a record attendance. No one disputed the fact that Ambercombe's church was in urgent need of extensive repairs. When George Aldridge proposed that a faculty be sought to sell its Georgian plate, normally kept in the bank at Westbridge, in order to raise the necessary funds, there was a general murmur of agreement, punctuated by hear hears from the Pyrford majority present. The opposition, headed by the Gillards and backed by a small group of elderly Ambercombe residents, failed to put forward any convincing alternatives. Moreover, it was handicapped by the deep booming support of Ethel Ridd, whose interventions provoked barely suppressed hilarity in some quarters. At one point Hugh Redshaw was seen to wipe his eyes. Finally the proposition, duly seconded, was carried by a large majority, and Robert Hoyle deftly damped down the situation by informing the meeting that the Consistory Court would certainly not hear the petition before the autumn, and took the next item on the agenda, the date and place of the Young Wives' Summer Outing.

During the early summer notices appeared in the porches of both churches announcing that objections to the petition had been lodged by Matthew Henry and Emily Margaret Gillard and Ethel Ridd, and that the Consistory Court of the diocese of Marchester would sit to hear the petition on 19 November. The remoteness of this date invested the situation with a sense of unreality, but like all distant dates it drew inexorably nearer and became suddenly imminent. There was a flurry of revived interest, and the proprietor of the Pyrford garage hurriedly organised a coach trip to Marchester for the occasion.

Wednesday 19 November was a still autumnal day of pale sunshine and early mists. A faint haziness penetrated the Chapter House of Marchester Cathedral, forming haloes round the pendant clusters of electric lights. The setting for the session of the Consistory Court was formal. An impressive oak chair on a dais under the magnificent east window awaited the Chancellor of the diocese. The dais was flanked by seating accommodation for legal representatives, the diocesan architect, an official of the company with which St John the Baptist's, Ambercombe, was insured, and the Archdeacon of Marchester, who supported the petition. Robert Hoyle, with George Aldridge and other officials of the Parochial Church Council, occupied one end of the front row of the public seats, and the two Gillards and some of their adherents the other. Ethel Ridd had elected to sit behind them. Parishioners of the humbler sort, overawed by their surroundings, had made for the back rows. Others, more assured, sat further forward at their ease. Bill Sandford clasped his hands behind his head and gazed around him with a sardonic expression. Hugh Redshaw shot meaningfully amused glances at any acquaintances whose eyes he could catch. His wife Miranda, a writer of verse for women's magazines, contemplated the east window, a tremulous smile on her lips. There was also a sprinkling of strangers, some interested, others with an hour or two to fill in. The central heating was efficient, and the atmosphere permeated with the soporific smell of warm ancient stone.

A sudden thunderous order to stand for the Chancellor of the Court brought the assembly hastily to its feet, dropping assorted property in the process and scrabbling to retrieve it. Escorted by the head verger and two members of his staff, a figure in barrister's wig and gown was escorted to the chair on the dais and took its seat. A pair of shrewd eyes in a face of eighteenth-century cast, full and impassive, surveyed the scene, and those present were instructed to sit down.

Very slowly the wheels of the judicial process set in motion by the parishioners of Pyrford-with-Ambercombe began to revolve. In the midst of a dead silence the Chancellor stated with extreme clarity the petition and its context, and identified those present in an official capacity.

'Let the plate in question be exhibited to the Court,' he concluded.

The posse of vergers who had remained standing by the door vanished, to return almost at once in procession, carrying various objects in the manner of figures in a frieze on a Greek vase.

'Hold them up please, so that they can be seen by everyone,' the Chancellor ordered. 'You will all see a Georgian silver-gilt chalice. It bears the date 1756, and has a cover designed to serve as a pyx. There is a matching set of cruets of the same date, and two Georgian candlesticks of hallmarked silver. These articles, the sum total of the plate in question, have collectively been valued by a representative of the eminent London firm of –'

The name of the eminent London firm was lost in an earsplitting screech of wood on stone.

'It's not all there!'

Ethel Ridd was on her feet, her deep bass voice reverberating through the Chapter House. There was a moment's paralysed silence, broken by the Chancellor.

'You are Ethel Ridd, and have lodged an Objection to the petition before the Court,' he said calmly. 'What is your status, please?'

'I was housekeeper to Father Viney.'

'I only need to know if you are married or single.'

'I'm single,' she replied impatiently, gripping the back of the chair in front.

'You are saying, Miss Ridd,' the Chancellor went on, after making a note of her statement, 'that the former parish of St John the Baptist, Ambercombe, owns plate over and above what is in front of us here?'

'Yes, it does. There's another chalice.'

There was a lengthy pause, during which the Chancellor consulted various documents from the pile in front of him.

'I have here,' he informed the Court, 'the terrier, that is, the official list of the property owned by the parish of St John the Baptist, Ambercombe. It includes two chalices, the one being exhibited here today, and a Victorian chalice dated 1860, which I understand is in regular use. No application for permission to sell it has been made, so it has not been brought to the Court. Does this meet your point, Miss Ridd?'

'No, it doesn't,' she replied truculently. ''Tisn't the ordinary one I'm talking about. It's the little one Father Viney'd use in and out for Saints' days. It had jewels stuck in it.'

In the breathless silence the Chancellor put down his pen, folded his hands and looked at her steadily. Then his gaze moved to Margaret Gillard.

'I understand, Mrs Gillard, that for some years before the amalgamation of the two benefices, you held the office of churchwarden at Ambercombe?'

24

Embarrassed at being directly addressed she half rose to her feet.

'That's right, sir.'

'You need not stand. As churchwarden you will have represented the parish at the Archdeacon's Visitations, and have had an accurate knowledge of the church's property?'

'Yes, sir.'

'How many chalices does it possess?'

'Two, sir. The one that's here now, and the one that's always used except for the festivals. I've never seen any other. I –'

'I can't help who's seen it and who hasn't,' Ethel Ridd interrupted loudly and angrily. 'I only know as I have.'

'Thank you, Mrs Gillard.' The Chancellor redirected his attention to Ethel Ridd.

'When did you last see this third chalice?' he asked her.

'Feast of St Barnabas last year. Father Viney's Patronal he used to call it. We had a Mass eleven o'clock, same as usual for Saints' days. The day he was taken.'

'The Feast of St Barnabas is on the eleventh of June,' the Chancellor informed the Court. 'Who besides yourself was in church, Miss Ridd?'

She gave a sniff.

'Nobody from the village. There never was weekdays. There was a hiker came in. They often do, to look round the church, but he didn't stop, seeing there was a service on.'

There was a pause, during which the Chancellor studied her thoughtfully.

'Assuming that you are not mistaken, Miss Ridd, about a third chalice sometimes being used by the late Mr Viney,' – he raised an authoritative hand to check her indignant interruption – 'and in view of the fact that there is no official record of its existence as church property, I can only assume that it was a personal possession of Mr Viney, so this Court is not concerned with it.'

'Well then, it's been stolen, and that's flat,' Ethel Ridd replied angrily. 'Who's taken it? There was no chalice in with his bits of things.'

She glanced aggressively behind her, and an indignant murmur was audible from the back rows. Archdeacon Lacy turned to Robert Hoyle, his enquiring eyebrows shooting up to a positively fantastic level. Then, in a hostile silence, she stalked out of the Chapter House. As she did so a reporter from the *Westbridge Evening News* slipped unobtrusively from his seat and followed her.

Unmoved, the Chancellor directed the head verger to remove the plate to a place of safety, and called on the diocesan architect to report on the fabric of Ambercombe church.

From now on the hearing became progressively more technical, and there was a tendency for the general public to get restive. After the adjournment for lunch, only those required to give evidence presented themselves. Finally, at a quarter past five, the Chancellor announced that he was in possession of all the information he required, and that he would deliver judgment in due course. Rising to his feet, he declared the enquiry closed, and made a dignified exit with his escort of vergers. There were hasty confabulations among those who had been obliged to stay the whole course.

'Home and dry, I think,' the Archdeacon remarked rather abstractedly to Robert Hoyle. 'I'll be in touch with you if anything crops up.'

In Pyrford and Ambercombe indignation against Ethel Ridd supplanted the vexed question of the sale of the plate as the topic of the day. It was fanned by a paragraph hastily inserted in the Stop Press column of the *Westbridge Evening News*, sensationalising the allegedly missing chalice. Feeling ran high, and no one was surprised that she appeared to be keeping out of the way on the following day, Thursday 20 November.

The publicity aroused interest in the two villages, and late in the season though it was, a few curious visitors arrived by car and wandered around. On Friday morning Margaret Gillard was fetched from a bi-weekly bread-making session in her kitchen by someone knocking on the Barton's front door. Hastily wiping flour from her hands in some irritation she went to open it, and found a middle-aged couple armed with an order from a firm of Westbridge estate agents to view the vicarage.

'We're househunting,' the woman told her, 'and thought

Ambercombe looked so attractive in the *Evening News* photograph yesterday. But we can't find the caretaker to let us have the key.'

'I think she must be away,' her husband said. 'There are milk bottles and papers outside her cottage. We're sorry to bother you, but wondered if the key had been left here by any chance?'

The situation revived Margaret Gillard's anger with Ethel Ridd.

'No, it hasn't,' she replied. 'It's too bad of Miss Ridd to go off without pinning a notice on her door about the key. I can't let you into the vicarage, but I'll take you along and show you what I can from outside if you like, seeing you've come all this way.'

The offer was accepted gratefully, and snatching a coat from a peg, she led the couple along the road and through the churchyard into the vicarage garden. The unexpected sight of some open windows greeted them.

'Well, I never!' she exclaimed. 'It looks as though Miss Ridd's over here instead of at her own place. I can't make it out.'

Margaret Gillard was perfectly correct in her surmise. The front door was unlocked, and on going into the house they found Ethel Ridd lying on the kitchen floor. An ugly discoloration on the back of her head had stained the thin strands of her grey hair.

Chapter 2

Conditioned to emergencies by the day-to-day life of a farm and conscious of her status as a churchwarden, Margaret Gillard acted decisively. To her relief the househunting couple, now identified as a Mr and Mrs Brand of Westbridge, showed no signs of panic. At her request Mr Brand hurried off to dial 999 from the Barton and report the finding of the body to the police, and subsequently to locate her husband, out somewhere on the farm. Her own duty was obviously to stay on the spot and ensure that nothing was touched. Mrs Brand began to look a little green, and Margaret took her by the arm and led her firmly to a garden seat, keeping up a flow of reassuring conversation. As she talked, a jumble of thoughts and surmises jostled for priority just below the surface of her mind. After what seemed an eternity but was actually a bare ten minutes, there came heavy running footsteps, and Matthew Gillard burst into the vicarage garden from the churchyard, followed by a breathless Mr Brand. After he had been briefed, the conversation dwindled to an exchange of disconnected remarks as they waited with ears strained for the approach of a police car. At last Matthew leapt to his feet.

'Car coming up the hill,' he said. 'You'd best all wait here. I'll go out to the church gate.'

He had hardly reached it when a car came into sight and braked to a halt at his signal. Detective-Inspector Frost of the Westbridge CID, a massive six-footer of surprising agility, emerged simultaneously and introduced himself and his sergeant who was at the wheel.

'Was it you who rang us, sir?' he asked.

'No. I'm Matthew Gillard of Ambercombe Barton down the road there, on the left. It was my wife found the body, when she took a couple who'd come househunting over to see the vicarage. She thought she ought to stay on the spot, and sent the gentleman to ring you and find me. They're all three waiting in the garden. Shortest way's through the churchyard here.'

He led the procession of three, feeling both relieved and uneasily aware that all initiative was now out of his own hands, and in the impersonal ones of the police.

After congratulating Margaret Gillard on her presence of mind, and asking a few brief questions, Inspector Frost suggested that she and the Brands would be more comfortable waiting over at the Barton.

'Perhaps you'd stay here, sir,' he said to Matthew. 'There'll be information we'll be glad of.'

A few minutes later he looked up at the two men who were standing at the kitchen door while he examined the body.

'Stone dead,' he said tersely. 'Twelve hours at least, I'd say. Go over and ring for support, will you, Sarge?'

He got to his feet, dusting the knees of his trousers, and stared at length round the bare room with its rusty cooker and old-fashioned sink. There was no sign of a weapon, nor, he noted, of a handbag.

'Do you know her?' he asked Matthew Gillard.

'Sure,' the farmer replied. 'Ethel Ridd. She lives – lived – in the middle one of the three Quarry Cottages, a couple of minutes away. Used to be housekeeper to old Reverend Viney. He died last summer, rising ninety. Maybe you've heard of him? The parish is joined up with Pyrford now,' Matthew went on, getting an affirmative nod, 'and the diocese has put this up for sale. Ethel Ridd was caretaking in a manner of speaking. Opened the windows mornings and closed 'em up before dark, and showed over anybody wanting to view.'

Inspector Frost nodded again. 'What about her next of kin? Are there any locally?'

'Not that I know of – not in these parts, I'm pretty sure. Maybe my wife's heard her mention somebody.'

'Secluded sort of place this vicarage,' the Inspector commented. 'Easy enough to get in with windows open all day, and nobody around. Do you get a lot of chaps sleeping rough in these parts?'

'Not this time of year, we don't. Summertime they fetch up at my place now and again and ask for a job. They're after a handout, of course, and I see 'em off smart. Let the dogs play up. They soon clear out.'

Inspector Frost glanced round as Sergeant Hill reappeared at the front door, and turned to Matthew Gillard again.

'I'd be glad if you'd take Sergeant Hill over to the deceased lady's cottage, Mr Gillard. I shouldn't think she'd have locked it up, just to slip across here. See if anything's been disturbed, Sarge.'

Getting into the vicarage wouldn't have been any problem whatever with windows open, he thought, as their footsteps died away. The kitchen window itself seemed a likely bet, being round at the back of the house. The way she'd fallen with her arms forward looked as though she'd been reaching up to shut it when she was hit from behind. There might be traces of mud under the body, and on the ground outside – jobs for the boys when they turned up. No problem about clearing out either. She'd probably have left the front door open while she did her shutting-up round.

In confirmation of these ideas he found clear traces of mud on the stone floor of a dank little scullery leading off the kitchen. They were behind the door, and there was a clear view both of the body and of the window behind it through the gap at the hinges. Even more satisfactory was the discovery that half a brick had been removed from the disintegrating fireplace under an ancient copper for boiling washing. Fragments of mortar and brickdust on the floor indicated that the removal was recent.

His investigations were broken off at this point by the return of Sergeant Hill and Matthew Gillard. The former reported that Ethel Ridd's cottage had been unlocked, with the key on the inside of the front door. This opened into a combined kitchen–living room which showed no signs of having been disturbed. There was a handbag on the table. He had locked up and brought away the key. No one was at home at number 3, and the first one in the row was obviously shut up.

'That one belongs to a Marchester doctor,' Matthew Gillard said. 'He uses it weekends in and out, and for holidays. The third one's Mr Sandford's. He's a lecturer at Westbridge College of Education, and out a lot.'

Inspector Frost reflected that it was not going to be easy to find witnesses of Ethel Ridd's final trip to the vicarage. He thanked Matthew Gillard for his help, and asked him to wait with his wife and Mr and Mrs Brand at the farm.

'I'll be over to take your statements as soon as my chaps turn up and get started here,' he said. 'They should be along soon now.'

He had hardly shown Sergeant Hill his discoveries in the scullery when his support materialised, together with the Westbridge police surgeon, Dr Moffatt. While the photographer and fingerprint experts assembled their apparatus, Dr Moffatt examined the body, keeping up a running commentary as he did so.

'Killed instantly, from the look of it. A terrific swipe with a dear old blunt instrument. She hadn't even turned her head ... No chicken, of course ... probably a bit deaf ... grit or something on what hit her, embedded in the wound, for the lab boys to get busy on, anyway, if you haven't found the weapon ... off the cuff, about forty to fifty hours ago, but I might be able to narrow it down when I've had a proper look at her.'

'That takes us back to Wednesday afternoon or evening,' Inspector Frost calculated, 'and ties up with what the farmer chap from down the road told us about her habits. She was caretaking this place and came over mornings and evenings to open windows and shut 'em again.'

Dr Moffatt agreed that the late afternoon of Wednesday made sense.

'No money on her, and nothing in the way of a watch or brooch. Looks like some drop-out to me, who'd got in to spend a night under cover, and decided to cash in when the poor old girl turned up. When shall I send along the mortuary van?'

This matter being settled, he hurried off. Inspector Frost set his technicians to work on the kitchen and scullery while Sergeant Hill went over the rest of the house for any further signs of the murderer's presence.

'Take a look outside, too,' he said. 'It seems plain enough that somebody got in through a window.'

*

At Ambercombe Barton the warm kitchen where the Gillards and Brands awaited him was a welcome change from the fusty vicarage. He gladly accepted a cup of coffee, took a short statement from the Brands, and let them go with apologies for the delay.

'I'll have to take up a bit more of your time, I'm afraid,' he said, on settling down again with the Gillards. 'There'll be a post-mortem on Miss Ridd, but unofficially the police surgeon puts her death back to Wednesday afternoon or evening. Do either of you know anything about her movements on Wednesday?'

They both looked up sharply, and Margaret, quicker off the mark than her husband, spoke first.

'Ethel Ridd was alive and well in Marchester Chapter House Wednesday morning,' she said. 'Wednesday was right out of the ordinary for quite a few Pyrford and Ambercombe people. I daresay you read about the Consistory Court case over our church plate up here?'

'I did see a headline in the evening paper,' Inspector Frost replied, 'but I don't know much about it, and that's a fact. If you think it can have any bearing on Miss Ridd's death, perhaps you'd fill me in a bit?'

He listened attentively to the Gillards' account of the court proceedings, trying to assess their relevance, if any, to his case.

'You say Miss Ridd's remark in court about somebody having stolen this chalice put local people's backs up?' he asked.

'I'll say it did,' Matthew Gillard replied. 'Down at the Stars last night the whole bar was still going on about it. Everybody took it she meant somebody local had pinched the thing.'

'Can you see anybody being so mad with her for blurting that out that they'd hide up in the vicarage and bash her head in?'

Both Gillards expostulated vehemently. There wasn't a soul in the place who'd do such a thing.

'And what's more,' Matthew added, 'it's a lot of baloney about a chalice with jewels stuck in it, isn't it, Maggie? You

32

were churchwarden for ten years and more, and know well enough what plate there was.'

Margaret Gillard concurred, and gave it as her opinion that Ethel Ridd had religious mania of a sort, and must have dreamt up the chalice.

'I don't mean she was round the bend,' she said, 'but she and old Mr Viney were proper cranks about the old monks who built the church hundreds of years ago.'

Inspector Frost felt that the chalice, real or imaginary, was a dead end, and embarked on another topic.

'How and when would Miss Ridd have got back here from Marchester?' he asked.

By bus to Pyrford, the Gillards thought. They'd given her a lift in. There was a bus out of Marchester at midday, and another at three. The run took just under an hour and a quarter. Then she'd walk up the hill to Ambercombe.

This ought to be easy enough to check, Frost thought, making a note.

'If the sort of vagrant was around who'd get into an empty house and attack an elderly woman, he'd surely have been seen by somebody?' he said.

'That sort find their way up here from Pyrford,' Matthew told him. 'They thumb lifts along the road, try scrounging in the village, and then come on to Ambercombe. Seems funny nobody's come forward about seeing a chap.'

'Through Pyrford's not the only way of getting here, is it? Where does the road outside lead to?'

It soon became not much more than a lane, he learnt, passing one or two farms, and finally coming out on a road from Marchester going round the Whitehallows on the north side. There was a track over the hills hikers sometimes used in summer, but hoboes wouldn't come that way. It was just rough heath used for summer grazing. Nothing up there for the likes of them.

'I take it you were both at the court in Marchester on Wednesday,' Frost said, making more notes. 'Was anybody about here?'

'The house was shut up,' Margaret Gillard replied. 'We fixed for the children – they're at the Westbridge Comprehensive – to get off the school bus and stay with friends down at Pyrford till we picked them up. We didn't get back before half past six. What about the men, Matt?'

It appeared that the farm hands were working with the tractor in a distant field all the morning, but the cowman and a helper would have been around for the afternoon milking. Frost took names and addresses. He then asked Margaret if she knew anything about Ethel Ridd's next-of-kin, but she replied that she had never heard Ethel Ridd mention any relatives.

'One more thing, and I needn't bother you any further for the moment,' he said. 'My sergeant'll take statements from you later. When does that neighbour of Miss Ridd's, Mr – Mr Sandford, isn't it, get home from work? He might be able to give us some information about Wednesday afternoon and evening.'

Frost surprised a grin on Matthew Gillard's face. Margaret clicked her tongue, but obviously in merely token disapproval.

'Gay bachelor?' he queried.

'Free and easy,' Matthew replied. 'He wasn't working Wednesday, if that's what you're thinking. He's a part-timer, and Wednesday isn't one of his days. I saw him sitting in the Chapter House at the hearing, and he gave me a wink. Before the lunch break, that was. What he did afterwards, and whether he slept in his own bed Wednesday night, I wouldn't know. I don't remember hearing him coming back, but we were late getting in ourselves, as Margaret was saying. Mondays, Tuesdays and Fridays are his regular West-bridge days, but I daresay he'll be off somewhere for the weekend.'

On returning to the vicarage Frost found the routine investigation in full swing. To his satisfaction, traces of mud similar to those in the scullery had been found under Ethel Ridd's body, just in front of the kitchen window, and samples of both had been collected for analysis. The ground outside the window was unfortunately hard, but some faint impressions had been photographed. Frost left his technicians engaged in the unpromising task of trying to bring up fingerprints on the flaking paintwork of the window frame, and returned to his car to plan the various lines of enquiry that would have to be followed up. It looked like some vagrant, true enough, but you couldn't take things at their face value like that. A lot of the locals would know the deceased's routine. There'd have to be a check-up on where people had been on Wednesday afternoon and evening. A tiresome time-consuming job, needing a hell of a lot of manpower, and they were stretched as it was ... The Super would blow his top when he heard how things were.

Chapter 3

The swift passage of a police car through Pyrford, and on up
the hill to Ambercombe, was an immediate talking point
for people who chanced to see it. The follow-up by a second
car bringing the technicians, with the police surgeon's Austin
Maxi on its tail, brought small groups out on to the village
green. They speculated excitedly, and stood gazing towards
the north-east in the manner of the spectators of Halley's
Comet in the Bayeux Tapestry. Suddenly a bread delivery
van came in sight, bucketing recklessly down from Ambercombe. Its driver, hardly able to wait to deliver the sensational news of Ethel Ridd's murder, brought the van to a
shuddering halt and vaulted to the ground. He was immediately surrounded by eager questioners.

The mounting buzz of conversation attracted the attention
of James Morse of the Old Forge, a retired chartered ac-
countant and secretary of the Parochial Church Council. He
came out of his house to discover what was happening.

'I bet that officious blighter Aldridge has got on to Hoyle,'
he remarked to his wife, on returning home and breaking
the news to her. 'All the same, I think I'll give him a ring.'

The only reply from the Rectory was the ringing tone. It
was not until mid-afternoon that he succeeded in contacting
Robert Hoyle, who, with his wife, had been lunching with
friends in Westbridge. His reaction on hearing of the murder
was an incredulous horror.

'Good God!' he exclaimed. 'How absolutely appalling. I
suppose some half-crazy homeless type must have followed
her in ... I can imagine her threatening anybody like that,
you know ... I'd better go straight up ... No, on second
thoughts, I'll let the Archdeacon know first. Thanks most
awfully for ringing, James.'

In his turn, Archdeacon Lacy reacted with a horrified
exclamation. It was followed by so long a silence that Robert

Hoyle, his mind already reaching out to problems ahead, finally cleared his throat impatiently.

'My dear chap, I can't tell you how sorry I am you've been landed with this frightful situation,' Eric Lacy said hurriedly. 'It's difficult to take it in ... You say the police are in action?'

'Carloads of them, apparently. I thought I'd go up right away, as soon as I'd rung you.'

'Absolutely right. They're bound to want to see you, anyway, as it's happened on church property, unfortunately ... Keep me posted, and let me know if I can help in any way at all. If it's any comfort you'll find people will forget their differences and pull together in the face of a disaster like this.'

After a hasty consultation with his wife, Robert Hoyle got out his car again and started off. He raised a hand in sombre greeting to various Pyrford parishioners, but drove straight through the village and headed for Ambercombe. The prospect of the inevitable publicity gave him a prickling sensation at the back of his neck. A horrific vision of Ethel Ridd's funeral took shape in his mind.

Three police cars were drawn up at the church gate, watched from a safe distance by a small group of Ambercombe residents. As Robert parked alongside and got out, a tall burly figure in plain clothes came down the churchyard path and gave him a searching look. Apparently his dog collar served to identify him.

'Reverend Hoyle, sir? I'm Detective-Inspector Frost of Westbridge, in charge of this enquiry. I take it you know what's happened? I'd be glad of a word with you, if it's convenient.'

'Certainly,' Robert replied. 'I've only just got back from Westbridge, or I'd have been here before.'

'What I'm hoping you can do to start off with, is to give us some information about Miss Ridd's next-of-kin,' Inspector Frost said, as soon as they were settled in the police car. 'From what Mr and Mrs Gillard say, she doesn't seem to be a local woman.'

'Sorry, Inspector, but I can't help you at all over this. I've only been here since March, and the situation up here was – well, decidedly unusual, in the previous incumbent's time. Do you know all about it, or shall I fill you in?'

'Please do, sir.'

'Would you say Miss Ridd was of sound mind?' Frost asked, when Robert's statement came to an end.

'That's a dicey question about quite a lot of people, isn't it? My reaction is to say, yes, she was. Eccentric, certainly, and a figure of fun in the parish, but she was perfectly capable of coping with day-to-day life, and taking on a small job like caretaking at the vicarage. Her eccentricity arose from the fact that she'd become infected by Mr Viney's obsession with his church's past. I think she saw him as a sort of twentieth-century reincarnation of the Tadenham Abbey monks who built the church, and herself as a sort of lay brother, if you get me.'

'Sounds a rum sort of set up to me,' Frost commented, looking baffled. 'Still, I catch your drift, I think. Going back to Miss Ridd, had she any personal enemies that you know of?'

'None that I know of. As I said just now, people were indignant at her remark in the Consistory Court that this chalice she declared she'd seen must have been stolen. But it's fantastic to think that anybody would feel strongly enough about it to murder her. Surely' – Robert paused briefly – 'it points to some down-and-out who'd got into the vicarage, and lost his head when she walked in on him? One of those rootless unstable types.'

'I'll grant you that it could well be,' Frost conceded, 'but we can't just write off the locals, you know. There must be quite a few people who knew her routine, for instance. We'll have to check up on where everybody was on Wednesday afternoon and early evening. Seeing you're here, sir, and we're both busy people, perhaps we might start off with yourself?'

Robert Hoyle was fleetingly outraged. Then he grinned cheerfully.

'Fair enough, Inspector. I was at the Consistory Court hearing in the Marchester Cathedral Chapter House from two o'clock until about a quarter to six. The Chancellor rose at a quarter past five, but I stayed for a word with the Archdeacon and one or two other people. Mr Morse, our PCC secretary, gave me a lift both ways, and I got home at about twenty to seven. He lives at the Old Forge in Pyrford.'

'Thank you, sir. That should be two residents crossed off the list. Who else local was in court up to the end of the proceedings?'

As he jotted down names the sound of an approaching car made Frost look up.

'First of the press gentlemen,' he remarked sardonically. 'Ted Joynt of the *Westbridge Evening News*. Wonder he's been so slow off the mark. Leave this one to me, sir. About the inquest, it'll be Monday morning, in Westbridge. I'll ring you when the time's fixed. It'll be adjourned, of course, but the coroner'll issue a burial certificate. If no relatives turn up, it'll be up to the people of the parish if they want to make the funeral arrangements, seeing that the deceased's a parishioner of long standing.'

'I'm quite sure the parish will want to be responsible,' Robert said. 'I'd better attend the inquest myself, and say so officially.'

At Ambercombe Barton he was warmly received by the Gillards, and reflected that Eric Lacy had been right about the reconciling effect of local disasters. The controversial issue of the sale of Ambercombe church plate had apparently shrunk to insignificance. It was settled that Margaret Gillard should accompany him to the inquest.

'As to expense, we don't want any Social Security taking over the poor thing's funeral,' she said decisively. 'We'll have it all done properly. People'll be glad to give. The WI'll go round for subscriptions, if she didn't put by for her burial in her lifetime, that is, and there'll be a wreath, of course. You leave all that to me, Mr Hoyle. You'll have plenty else to see to.'

Somewhat heartened by this evidence of good emerging from evil, Robert Hoyle shortly afterwards started for home. On the way down he had to draw in to let the mortuary van pass, and this brought back his sense of incredulity. Why, only a few hours ago he and Jean had been enjoying a good lunch with old friends. In retrospect it seemed like another world.

A strange car was drawn up at the front door of the Rectory, and he was seized with foreboding, immediately realised by finding Jean being cornered by a reporter. Firmly resisting an impulse to kick the man and his notebook out of the house, he was deliberately friendly and co-operative. But while he made considered replies to loaded questions, he realised only too well that nothing he said would prevent the whole tragic affair being grotesquely sensationalised. This was borne out by a series of telephone calls from various parishioners in the course of the evening. These confirmed his worst apprehensions. It appeared that the bar of the Seven Stars was so crowded that patrons had to overflow on to the village green. The press had turned up in force, and memories were being stimulated by free drinks on expense accounts.

'Believe it or not, my dear chap,' Hugh Redshaw reported in a tone of sophisticated amusement, 'they're muck-raking about Ethel Ridd and old Barny Viney. Rich, isn't it?'

'Nauseating to my mind,' Robert replied briefly.

'Of course, dear boy, of course, but it's these chaps' living, poor devils. We literary hacks, you know ... And if you'd ever *seen* old Barny ...'

In the middle of a late supper Robert suddenly put down his knife and fork and stared at his wife.

'George Aldridge didn't come round or ring while I was up at Ambercombe, did he?'

Jean shook her head.

'He couldn't have. I was in the whole time.'

'It's just struck me that he simply hasn't surfaced. It's extraordinary, when you think how he tries to blow up the smallest thing to do with the parish into a major issue, and always with a sort of power-sharing implication.'

'It *is* odd,' Jean agreed. 'I suppose he can't be ill, or anything? He could have rung, anyway. I wonder if –'

The Rectory telephone rang yet again. This time, however, it was the unexpected excitement of a call from their son Thomas, in his first term at Oxford. This welcome distraction and the need to reconsider various parish arrangements for the weekend temporarily drove George Aldridge's unusual behaviour from Robert Hoyle's mind. In bed that night, however, it recurred to him. Didn't Christian charity require a call at the Village Stores to see if anything was amiss with the Aldridges? He was almost asleep when another thought which had been niggling unnoticed suddenly surfaced. What was the Archdeacon thinking during his lengthy silence on first hearing the news of Ethel Ridd's death? Sleep finally supervened, putting an end to speculation.

At an early hour on Saturday morning a full-scale police investigation got under way, and was to pursue its relentless course throughout the weekend. One aspect was a thorough search for any report or trace of vagrants in the neighbourhood of Pyrford and Ambercombe during the week. There was a house-to-house enquiry. Special attention was given to outlying farms, and barns and other outbuildings were searched. Bus drivers and other known road users were questioned. Requests for information went out from the local radio station and were conspicuously displayed by the *Westbridge Evening News* and other regional newspapers.

Simultaneously the checking of people's movements on Wednesday afternoon and evening was carried out. Under Inspector Frost's methodical direction the information gathered was carefully analysed and listed, in readiness for a conference with the Chief Constable and Detective-Superintendent Canning after the adjourned inquest on Ethel Ridd on Monday morning.

The three men met in the Super's office at Westbridge police headquarters, all looking decidedly jaded. Ethel Ridd's murder had by no means been their sole preoccupation over the weekend.

'Well, what does all this stuff of yours add up to, Frost?' Colonel James Greenaway, Chief Constable of Whiteshire, asked wearily.

Red-eyed from lack of sleep, Inspector Frost was succinct.

'Precious little sir, I'm afraid. We've combed the district

without finding a sign of a vagrant around. Every adult in both villages has been interviewed about his or her whereabouts from midday last Wednesday and we've got 'em all down on one of these three lists.'

The CC put out a hand for the typewritten sheets.

'List A: persons known to have been away from the area,' he read aloud. 'List B: persons in the area with their movements vouched for. List C: persons in the area giving unsupported statements of their movements ... God, I'd no idea there were so many people in those ruddy villages ... A good effort of yours and your chaps in the time, Frost.'

'Thank you, sir. That's as far as we got, I'm afraid. For what it's worth, we haven't found a shred of evidence that any of these people had what you might call a personal link with the deceased.'

'Did you get the feeling they were holding back on you?' Superintendent Canning asked.

'No, we didn't. Trouble was to stop 'em talking. She seems to have been a character. But there was a bit of feeling about her saying somebody'd pinched a chalice from Ambercombe church.'

'Well, unless there's a homicidal maniac in the parish, she'd hardly have been bumped off for that,' the CC remarked. 'Added to which, it seems the chalice doesn't exist according to the official records ... So what? It certainly looks like some drop-out going beserk. We'll keep the publicity going: something may still come in, especially from neighbouring areas. And I suppose we'd better follow up those people who can't produce supporting evidence on where they claim to have been at the time of the murder. Though how we're going to find the manpower, I don't know. We're over-stretched as it is. I –'

The buzzer on the desk suddenly interrupted him. Superintendent Canning flicked a switch.

'What is it?' he barked.

'The Archdeacon of Marchester's here, sir. He wants to see Inspector Frost, or someone in authority who's on the Ambercombe case.'

The three men exchanged surprised glances.

'Better have him up,' the CC said, on being appealed to.

'What it's in aid of, God only knows, but the chap's not a crank: I can vouch for that.'

A few moments later Eric Lacy, carrying a folder, was ushered in.

'Do sit down, Archdeacon,' Colonel Greenaway said, after carrying out introductions. 'We're actually discussing this business at Ambercombe at the moment.'

'Thanks,' Eric Lacy replied, accepting a chair brought forward by Inspector Frost. 'I expect you're wondering why I've come in person, instead of ringing you. Well, the short answer is that I thought I'd have a better chance of being listened to ... Shall I go ahead?'

'Please do.'

'Can I take it that you know about the late Ethel Ridd's outburst in the Consistory Court last Wednesday morning?'

'You can,' Colonel Greenaway replied. 'We've got what we're taking to be an accurate report from the Reverend Robert Hoyle and others, and we also know that there's no official record of this chalice she was referring to.'

'This is really what I've come along about.' Eric Lacy told him, crossing his legs and leaning back in his chair. 'In my opinion the chalice did exist, and still does, I sincerely hope, unless some vandal's melted it down by now.'

His audience stared at him blankly.

'Of course!' Colonel Greenaway reacted suddenly. 'I've got there! You're an antiquarian, aren't you? An authority on church plate? Do you mean that you've got tangible evidence that this chalice is – or was – a reality?'

'It's like this,' Eric Lacy replied. 'The moment that unfortunate woman leapt to her feet and challenged the Chancellor, I knew that somewhere and at some time I'd come across a relevant fact. Ever since, I've been trying to track it down, but I didn't succeed until last night. It was a footnote in a book on the dissolution of the monasteries under Henry VIII. Tadenham Abbey was one of them, of course, and Ambercombe was one of its manors. The monks built the church, in fact. Tadenham surrendered to the Crown in 1538, and according to established procedure the Abbey valuables were listed, as a preliminary to being deposited with a chap called the Master of the King's Jewel House. These takeovers weren't a free-for-all, by any means. Careful records were kept, although there are occasional gaps. Tadenham's greatest treasure was a medieval chalice.' Eric Lacy paused, and surveyed his attentive audience. 'It was listed as five and three-eighths inches high, of silver-gilt, and set with precious stones. Well, you can see what's coming: it never reached the King's Jewel House. An immediate enquiry was ordered, but unfortunately one of the few gaps in the records occurs here – perhaps significantly – and there's no further reference to the matter.'

A complete silence of several moments' duration followed, during which Colonel Greenaway directed a long hard look at Eric Lacy.

'Is it likely that either Mr Viney or Miss Ridd had come on this reference to the chalice, and that she could have imagined seeing it in use?' he asked.

'A fair question. I posed it to myself. I can only say that the book containing the footnote wasn't on Barnabas Viney's shelves. I went to the sale of his things, and had a good look at his library, such as it was. I've never seen the reference anywhere else, and he certainly never mentioned the chalice to me.'

'If Miss Ridd hadn't merely heard of it at secondhand, then I suppose it must follow that she actually saw it, or one very like it,' Colonel Greenaway propounded cautiously. 'Just what's in your mind Archdeacon?'

'I think it's quite likely that the Tadenham monks buried it, hoping for better days. If they did, their own land at Ambercombe would have been a suitable place, perhaps very near the church. We don't know what heads rolled, if any, when the chalice wasn't forthcoming, but the record of the hiding place may well have been lost.'

'And the late Mr Viney may have dug it up, you suggest?'

Eric Lacy was unperturbed by the note of cynicism which he rightly interpreted as a defensive measure.

'This is speculation, I admit, but in the light of Miss Ridd's remarks, I think it's a possibility that he *did* find the chalice. That he froze on to it in complete secrecy seems quite in keeping with his outlook. He would have realised that it was a pre-Reformation piece, and seen it as a tangible link with the past that he practically lived in.'

Superintendent Canning shifted on his chair, frowning heavily, and struggled to establish some definite fact.

'This chalice, sir, if it's still around somewhere, would it be a very valuable piece?'

'Very valuable indeed, Superintendent, assuming that the description in the archives is correct. An interesting point is that the jewels are not described as counterfeit, as was often the case, so presumably they were genuine ... Well, gentlemen, I hope you don't feel that I've been wasting your time. But quite apart from this Ambercombe tragedy, it has occurred to me that there could be some link between the Tadenham chalice and these two other plate robberies in the diocese.'

The Chief Constable stiffened slightly.

'Which the police have so far completely failed to clear up, in fact?'

'No criticism was intended, Colonel. Well, I'll be getting along. Thank you for listening to me so patiently.'

When Inspector Frost returned from escorting the Archdeacon to his car, he found the Chief Constable hunched in thought, and Superintendent Canning tactfully silent. He returned unobtrusively to his own chair, and waited.

'Where we left off,' Colonel Greenaway said suddenly, 'was wondering how the hell we were going to find the chaps to follow up your List C, Frost. Now we've got these bloody plate robberies surfacing again. If there's anything at all in this yarn of the Archdeacon's, I don't see that it can possibly link up with the woman's remarks in court. Nobody would have dashed straight off on the strength of them to start searching for the chalice in Ambercombe vicarage on the off-chance, and then smashed her head in when she turned up. It's nonsense. But there could be a link with the plate robberies.'

'Two jobs instead of one,' Superintendent Canning observed gloomily.

'Exactly. But there's a way out for us, you know.'

'Push the murder on to the Yard, sir?'

'Just that. How do you chaps feel about it? ... *Nem con,* judging from your faces.'

Chapter 4

Whistling softly, Detective-Superintendent Tom Pollard returned from being briefed by his Assistant Commissioner to his room at New Scotland Yard, and buzzed his secretary.

'Get me Inspector Toye, will you?' he said.

Within a few minutes Toye presented himself.

'We're for the midnight from Paddington to Westbridge,' Pollard told him. 'As far as I can make out, we've been detailed to track down the Holy Grail. There's an old woman with her head bashed in for good measure,' he added hastily, sensing some reservation at this flippant treatment of a sacred topic.

'They must be a poor lot down there if they can't clear up a run-of-the-mill job like that,' Toye commented severely.

Pollard hoisted his feet on to his desk.

'Sit down,' he said, 'and I'll pass on what I've just had from the AC, though it doesn't add up to a lot. What there is of it is right up your street as PCC stalwart, so take that snooty expression off your face. The murderee is a spinster of seventy-five, called Ethel Ridd. She'd been housekeeper to the late Barnabas Viney, who was vicar of Ambercombe, a minute village in Whiteshire, for fifty-two years, and who died in June 1974.'

Toye expressed further disapproval.

'It shouldn't be allowed, staying in one living all that time,' he said warmly. 'I don't hold with the parson's freehold, as they call it. Parsons ought to move on, like nonconformist ministers. What's happened to the Paul Report, I'd like to know?'

'I can answer that one. It's fetched up in a pigeon-hole somewhere. Now, if you could manage to give your mind to what I'm doing my best to tell you, when old Viney died, the diocesan authorities promptly amalgamated the parish with an adjoining one, called Pyrford. Ambercombe church

46

dates from the twelfth century, and as Viney didn't bother much about repairs, it now needs a packet spending on it. To raise the wind, there's been a move, especially among Pyrford people, to get a faculty for the sale of some of the Ambercombe church plate. The new joint PCC voted to petition the Consistory Court of the diocese – Marchester, that is – and the case was heard last Wednesday. You can imagine the sensation in court when the plate in question was exhibited, and Ethel Ridd leapt to her feet and insisted that a chalice with jewels stuck in it was missing. The presiding legal eagle consulted the records, and couldn't find any reference to such a chalice. He questioned a Mrs Gillard, who had been Viney's churchwarden for years, and she said she'd never seen anything of the sort, and knew nothing about it. Whereupon Ethel Ridd asserted that somebody must have stolen the chalice, and swept out. These were her last recorded words. She was found dead in Ambercombe vicarage, now empty and up for sale, on Friday morning. She used to go in each day to air the place. The P-M puts the time of death as Wednesday afternoon or early evening ... I say, you're held spellbound by all this, aren't you? I said you would be.'

Toye conceded that a case to do with church affairs might be interesting, and anyway a nice change from some of the jobs they'd had lately.

'But mightn't this chalice have been the old gent's personal property?' he asked.

'Exactly what I put to the AC just now. Apparently the legal eagle was hit by the same idea, but Ethel Ridd replied that it hadn't turned up among the Reverend Viney's things after his death, so it couldn't have been his own. It seems quite clear that she was considered highly eccentric by the locals, so the Westbridge CID came to the conclusion that the whole business of the chalice was her imagination, and wrote it off as far as any relevance to the murder went. However, there was a surprising development this morning. The Archdeacon of Marchester turned up with a rather curious bit of information. He's a well-known authority on church plate, and had found a reference to a chalice like the one Ethel Ridd described, and which – this is the important point – had a potential link with Ambercombe. This is the gist of what he told the Westbridge people ...'

As Toye listened to the recorded disappearance of the Tadenham Abbey chalice in 1538, and Archdeacon Lacy's theory of its subsequent history, his normally impassive face developed an expression of scepticism.

'But there's not a shred of reliable evidence in all this, sir,' he protested. 'It's just what the Archdeacon thinks, and pretty far fetched at that, to my mind. If this is why Westbridge have asked us to take over, I'd say they've got a nerve! Let 'em get on with the job of tracking down any vagrant or stranger who was around last Wednesday: a type who'd break into an empty house to get a roof for the night. They know the lie of the land, and we don't.'

Pollard crossed one leg over the other.

'Again, more or less what I said to the AC. His reaction was to push a list of robberies of church plate at me. I hadn't registered the fact, but they've been going up steadily over the past couple of years, and are interestingly selective. Apparently ecclesiastical high-ups are beginning to make indignant noises at the police failure to recover the swag. This is really why Westbridge is getting help. The AC and others think there's a remote chance that Ethel Ridd's murder could tie up with the thefts by way of the Tadenham chalice. It's to be a sort of dual purpose enquiry: a two for the price of one idea. Anyway, we're for it, old chap, and we'd better get cracking if we want to look in at home before we take off. Rustle up a *Who's Who*, will you? I want to check up on the Venerable Eric Lacy, Archdeacon of Marchester.'

On the following morning Pollard and Toye breakfasted at their hotel in Westbridge, and went straight to police headquarters for a conference with the Chief Constable, Superintendent Canning and Inspector Frost. Pollard at once sensed a discomfited atmosphere which he rightly put down to the failure to trace any vagrant or other dubious character in the Ambercombe area on the previous Wednesday. The tactful approach seemed to be to stress the Yard's interest in a possible link between Ethel Ridd's murder and the Tadenham chalice.

'It's a rum situation,' he said easily. 'I've never been involved in anything like it before, and don't mind admitting that I'm feeling a bit out of my depth at the moment. I know how hard-pressed you people are, but I can see us having to come back on you rather a lot.'

The atmosphere relaxed, and he was assured of the fullest co-operation at all levels. After further discussion it was settled that Inspector Frost should carry on the enquiries into any strangers noticed in the area during the past week, while Pollard and Toye digested the contents of his file and decided on their plan of campaign.

'By the way,' Pollard said, 'I've looked up Archdeacon Lacy. Obviously he's an expert on church plate, but what do you make of him as a person?'

'One simply must say that he inspires confidence,' Colonel Greenaway replied, with perceptible regret in his voice. 'He definitely hasn't got bees in the bonnet or even a one-track mind. I've been making discreet enquiries, and his stock's high in the Chapter, and he's generally thought of as a sound decent chap. You'll be going over to see him, I expect? A car's laid on for you, and a room here with a phone, of course.'

The conference broke up shortly afterwards, and Pollard and Toye installed themselves in their quarters with the file and a set of large-scale maps of the locality.

As the morning wore on Pollard stretched, clasped his hands behind his head, and eyed Toye quizzically.

'Had another think?' he enquired, indicating the litter of typescript, photographs and plans on the table.

Toye grinned a trifle sheepishly.

'Meaning that it's beginning to look as though there's no hobo to pull in?'

'This is it. Nobody can say Frost hasn't been thorough, and it's suggestive that there's absolutely nothing to report after they've been going it hard for three days.'

'It needn't mean there's anything in the chalice yarn, though.'

'True enough. And I don't think we can take this non-hobo idea any further until we've been over and vetted that vicarage ourselves. Let's go and have a snack and drive out there. The Archdeacon can wait till later.'

An hour later they ran into the outskirts of Pyrford. It was a still grey day of low cloud, and the landscape lay drained of colour. The dark bulk of the Whitehallow Hills loomed oppressively over the village, dwarfing it to insignificance. It appeared deserted.

'Men gone back to work, and the women all clearing up the meal or having a nice sit down,' Toye diagnosed.

They drove on up the hill, passed Ambercombe Barton, and drew up outside the church. Pollard surveyed it with keen interest.

'Don't let me go in, or I'll be there till dark,' he said. 'We can get to the vicarage through the churchyard, can't we?'

Overgrown by bushes at the far end they found a gate hanging drunkenly on one hinge, and made their way into a garden suffering badly from neglect and autumnal decay. Toye produced a key handed over by Inspector Frost, and unlocked the battered front door. A smell of dry rot assailed their nostrils.

'How old empty houses with no damp courses do stink,' Pollard remarked, making a rapid inspection of the ground floor rooms. He opened a musty cupboard under the stairs and stirred some old newspapers with the toe of his shoe, shutting the door hastily at the sight of a cockroach.

In the kitchen they forced up the window and let in some fresh air, and managed to work back the rusty cobwebby bolts of the door leading from the scullery into the back garden. The door itself was stuck fast, but Toye eventually managed to open it.

'That's a lot better,' Pollard said. 'One thing's certain, anyway. No murderer came in that way. Frost and his boys have been over everything here with a toothcomb, so we needn't bother about dabs and whatever.'

They examined the chalk outline marking the position of the body, and the ringed traces of footmarks on the stone flags behind the scullery door, and made a careful inspection of both rooms, but without discovering anything fresh. The ashes of long-dead fires had been raked out from under the

50

copper, together with fragments of brick and crumbs of mortar. Pollard took off his coat, rolled up his shirt sleeve, lay down on the floor with a grimace and felt inside the firebox itself.

'Nix,' he said. 'Wouldn't it have been super if the old boy had hidden the chalice in there?'

Getting up, he shook the soot and reddish brick dust from his arm and hand, and hopefully turned on the cold tap over the sink, but no water emerged.

'No hope of a wash,' he grumbled, and went over to sit on the windowsill. Toye propped himself against the sink.

'You know,' Pollard said thoughtfully, 'a chap who's sleeping rough gets pretty fly at sizing up the possibilities of squatting in an empty house. This one's got For Sale notices up, and the open windows would show that somebody was looking after it. We've Mrs Gillard's evidence that they were open on Friday morning, so it seems reasonable to assume that Ridd opened up as usual on Wednesday, probably before she went off to Marchester. Suppose you'd been a vagrant who chanced on this place sometime on Wednesday before she came back. What would you have done?'

'Got in by this window, had a look round, decided it would be better than nothing for the night, and gone to ground in that cupboard in the hall when I heard somebody coming along to shut up.'

'So would I, except that I'd have tried to find a less foul cupboard upstairs. But are you sure you wouldn't have wrenched a chunk of brick from under the copper, and hidden behind that door, and burst out to bash Ethel Ridd's head as she was shutting the window behind me here?'

'Quite sure,' Toye replied categorically. 'Not unless I was a homicidal maniac, that is. Why, she hadn't even got a handbag with her. There's a note in the file that hers was found in her cottage, with several pounds in cash in it.'

'OK,' Pollard said. 'I'm with you all the way. But somebody killed her. Why? Could it have been necessary for somebody to shut her mouth. What about? Just for purposes of argument, let's suppose that the chalice *did* turn up here, and this somebody had managed to pinch it. After Ridd blurted out about it in court, he might have felt it would be healthier to have her out of the way.'

Toye leant against the sink in silent consideration, owl-like behind his hornrims.

'It would have been quick work,' he said at last, 'getting back from Marchester ahead of her.'

'That could narrow things down rather usefully. And I think he would have to have been a local, to know Ridd's caretaking routine.'

'We've got that list of Inspector Frost's of locals who can't bring any evidence of where they were on Wednesday afternoon and evening.'

Pollard groaned.

'I suppose it's going to mean grilling the whole damn lot of 'em individually. And this is all pure theorising. If only we'd got one bit of concrete evidence that we're on the right track ... Hell, this window's murder all right. My bottom's numb,' he added, getting up and rubbing his posterior.

Quite suddenly he stopped, and stared at Toye.

'Look here, where do you suppose that the X of our theory hung about waiting for Ridd to turn up? Surely not in that foul dank scullery, with absolutely nowhere to sit? I'd have sat on the stairs. Comparatively comfortable, not overlooked by any window, and easy to hear anyone coming up to the house. Let's have a look.'

Toye picked up the torch and they went into the hall. The staircase, immediately facing the front door, was of stained wood, with a central strip of worn linoleum which it had not been thought worthwhile to take up for the sale of Barnabas Viney's effects. The short November day was closing in, and the hall was already dusky. Toye directed the beam of the torch on the bottom step.

'Higher,' Pollard said. 'More comfortable for your legs.'

It was on the third step from the bottom, on the left side going up, and close to the wall, that they found traces of reddish grit. With infinite care these were brushed into a sterile envelope, which was sealed and labelled for the forensic laboratory. Toye, always generous in his admiration of Pollard's achievements, was jubilant.

'Hold on to your hat,' Pollard cautioned. 'We shan't know till they've analysed the stuff and compared it with the grit in the wound. But I rather think X sat just there, and put the bit of brick down beside him while he waited. Surely he must have brought a weapon of some sort. Perhaps he thought something on the spot would be safer. Nothing to be traced back to him.'

They locked up the house and left, this time going down a short drive to a lane connecting the road with Quarry Cottages. Turning left, they found no sign of life at these. Ethel Ridd's had an official seal on the door, and the lecturer inhabiting the last one had obviously not yet returned from Westbridge. Beyond the cottages the lane became a cart track, deeply rutted and partly grassed over. Pollard and Toye went on as far as the quarry. In the half-light it was an eerie scene of now abandoned activity, with weird-looking pieces of rusting machinery and a stretch of still dark water.

'It's too dark to see where these paths lead,' Pollard said, as they retraced their steps. 'We'd better get back to West-bridge and hand this stuff in, and see if the Archdeacon is free to see us after supper . . . I must just see if the church is still open while you turn the car. Give me the torch a minute.'

He ran up the path and flashed the light into the tiny south porch. To his utter amazement a young girl was crouched in abject panic against the door, a massive key in her hand, her face deathly white.

'My dear child, I'm afraid I frightened you!' he exclaimed. 'I'm so sorry. It's only the police, you know. I expect you've come over to lock up the church, haven't you?'

A vestige of colour crept back into her cheeks.

'It's all right,' she said hastily and almost inaudibly. 'Mother forgot to do it earlier.'

Pollard's mind moved quickly.

'Are you Mrs Gillard's daughter?' he asked. 'She's one of the churchwardens, isn't she, and you must live at Amber-combe Barton, just down the road?'

'That's right. Did you want to see the church?' the girl asked, in an obvious attempt to regain her composure.

'It's a bit dark now, I'm afraid. I'll have to come another

time. I'll walk down to your house with you, and my colleague can follow on with the car.'

Disregarding an incoherent protest, he called out to Toye to pick him up at the farm, and set off, walking with long strides to keep up with the girl's hurrying steps. Her answers to his friendly questions were monosyllabic, and on arriving at the front gate she bolted into the house like a frightened rabbit, barely pausing to thank him.

'I can understand that I gave the kid a bit of a jolt after what's happened up here,' Pollard said, describing the incident to Toye. 'Odd, though, that she wasn't reassured by finding that we were coppers. Quite the reverse, I thought.'

Chapter 5

'They've promised to get the tests on the stuff done by tonight if they possibly can,' Pollard said, coming out of the Westbridge police station and joining Toye in the car. 'Meanwhile I've dodged Frost. Even if there's a positive result it'll be risky to call off his hobo hunt. It would alert the Sitter on the Stairs right away.'

On arriving in Marchester they had a meal in the grill room of the Cathedral Hotel, and afterwards presented themselves punctually at eight-thirty for their appointment with Eric Lacy. Pollard had made a determined effort to bring an open mind to the encounter, but quickly found himself in agreement with the Chief Constable's assessment of the Archdeacon. Here was a scholar, obviously, but someone far removed from what most people understood by the word. This was an alive chap with plenty of humour and common sense.

Eric Lacy settled his visitors in comfortable chairs in his study, and supplied them with drinks.

'Well,' he said, sitting down himself, 'I seem to have put the cat among the pigeons, don't I? But I found myself possessing various bits of information which seemed too relevant to the situation to be kept to myself. First of all, the historical evidence about the Tadenham chalice is beyond dispute. Then secondly, I am convinced that poor Ethel Ridd was talking about a chalice that she actually had seen. Thirdly, the unusual one she described corresponds remarkably closely with the Tadenham one, and fourthly, there is the territorial link between Tadenham Abbey and Ambercombe. Finally one might add that burying treasure when times are out of joint has been a practice all through history.'

'May we begin by taking you up on the word "unusual"?' Pollard asked.

'Certainly. Two things struck me about her description of

the chalice she had seen old Viney using on occasions. She said it was small. Pre-Reformation chalices often were. Only the celebrant of a mass received the consecrated wine as well as the bread. The large chalices we're accustomed to see in churches today for communicating the lay congregation would not as a rule have been in use. Then there was her statement that the one she saw "had jewels stuck in it". Now this is very interesting. The chaps who listed the monastic treasures for the Crown at the time of the Dissolution knew their job, and recognised "counterfeit gems" as they called them. The stones in the Tadenham chalice were not described as counterfeit, and so were presumably genuine, making the chalice extremely valuable. Hence, no doubt, the uproar when it didn't reach Henry's coffers.'

'Thank you,' Pollard said. 'That's all very clear. It seems to lead us to Ethel Ridd herself. All we've gathered about her so far is that she was seventy-five, considered eccentric, and had religious mania of a sort. Had you any personal knowledge of her?'

'Rather surprisingly, yes,' Eric Lacy replied. 'I take it you know about the set up at Ambercombe at the time of Barnabas Viney's death? Well, when the old boy died there were no surviving relatives, and – quite irregularly – only one churchwarden, a Mrs Gillard, whom you'll doubtless meet. I felt I must lend a hand, especially over business affairs, and so saw something of Ethel Ridd. I discovered that she had been evacuated to the area from the East End in 1939, become Barny's housekeeper, and stayed on ever since. She was perfectly *compos mentis* over matters of daily life, but quite uneducated. Her reading and writing were rudimentary. And the restricted sort of life she'd led at Ambercombe had cut her off from ordinary people to an extent that would make her seem eccentric, quite apart from the religious mania she'd caught from her employer. I'm telling you all this to make it clear that she simply couldn't have imagined the chalice she spoke of. She just hadn't the mental equipment.'

'This reference to the chalice that you came across, sir,' Toye asked, 'couldn't Mr Viney have found it, and talked to her about it?'

'Greenaway raised that same question, Inspector, and of course it can never be answered definitely one way or the other. But if he had come on it, I feel sure he would have shown it to me, knowing my interest in church plate. I doubt if he'd have let on if he'd dug up the chalice in his garden – that's another matter. But I used to go over to see him from time to time, and it's my opinion that he would have shown me the book if he'd had it. But it wasn't on his shelves after his death, and I've never seen the reference anywhere else.'

'What was the book?' Pollard enquired.

'A chatty unscholarly little effort called *Wessex Abbeys.* It was published in 1886 at his own expense by a man called Septimus Ponsonby. He seems to have been one of those nineteenth-century amateur antiquarians of independent means and with an urge to get into print. In some ways the book doesn't do him justice. He could read sixteenth- and seventeenth-century script, and had dipped into the Tadenham archives, but hadn't the know-how to make proper use of them. He just lifted odd bits here and there which he thought would interest his readers, like the disappearance of the chalice and the pet monkeys kept by an abbess. Here it is, if you'd care to have a look.'

It was a small octavo volume bound in red cloth, now much faded, with a gilt title. Pollard glanced through its pages, some of which were spotted with damp, while a few were uncut.

'Picked it up in a junk shop in Salisbury,' Eric Lacy said, as the book was handed back to him. 'I've checked the extract about the chalice with the Public Records Office. The Tadenham stuff is there, but has never been systematically dealt with. An interesting job waiting for somebody who's got the time.'

'About Barnabas Viney,' Pollard resumed after a pause, 'and your suggestion that he might have dug up the chalice in the vicarage garden. Was he a gardening type?'

'Oh, very much so, until he got too old and feeble. He saw growing your own food as part of the monastic way of life, like carpentry and basic building skills. There's quite a big kitchen garden behind the house. He was a vegetarian, incidentally, and I expect poor Ethel Ridd had to be one, too. An amazing old boy. Here's a photograph of him, taken a couple of years ago, when he'd done his half-century at Ambercombe.'

Toye drew his chair closer to Pollard's, and they studied the photograph with interest. It showed a very old but still arresting face, square and sunken, with protruding cheek bones and deep clefts running to the corners of an obstinate mouth. The chin was strong and slightly underhung. The eyes under bushy white brows were unexpectedly serene and kindly, with dark circles below them. Thin, unkempt white hair stuck out at random over the head, and formed shaggy sideburns.

'Reminds me of a picture of one of the prophets in Old Testament times,' Toye commented. 'I don't know, though. A bit too peaceful, perhaps.'

Eric Lacy gave him an approving glance.

'You're right there, Inspector. It was the peace of the monastic life and the time for prayer that appealed to him – mercifully. What he'd have been like, as a militant in the diocese, I tremble to think.'

'Let's suppose that Mr Viney actually did dig up the chalice in the vicarage garden,' Pollard said thoughtfully. 'Wouldn't you have expected Ethel Ridd to know about it? Yet I can't help feeling that if she did she would have blurted it out in court when the ownership of the alleged chalice was being discussed.'

Eric Lacy considered.

'I agree with you there,' he said, 'and I think it indicates that if he had dug it up he hadn't told her. There were no flies on old Barny, you know. He'd have realised that if the find came to the ears of the diocesan authorities they might have been able to make him hand the chalice over for safe-keeping. Not that I know what the legal position would be in a case like that. Then another thing is that Ethel Ridd was very limited mentally. Even if he had started using a chalice that she had never seen before, it might not have aroused her curiosity in any way. And of course there's the possibility that he might have made the find during his

58

early years at Ambercombe before she arrived in the place.'

'Yes, I see,' Pollard replied.

Another pause followed during which he turned over a number of matters in his mind. Mellow and resonant, the nine strokes of the hour from the cathedral clock hung in the air and died slowly away. He came to a decision.

'Mr Archdeacon, I think we should take you into our confidence, knowing that we can rely on your discretion ...'

As he listened to the account of the afternoon's investigations at Ambercombe vicarage, Eric Lacy's eyebrows shot up and descended again only very gradually. His long narrow face had a completely absorbed expression.

'But you know, Superintendent,' he said, when Pollard finished talking, 'if it turns out that you're right about the murderer needing to silence Ethel Ridd because he'd stolen the chalice, it narrows down the enquiry very considerably, doesn't it?'

Pollard looked at him enquiringly.

'I'm not sure that I'm with you.'

'Well, Ethel Ridd said that Viney used it in Ambercombe church on the morning of the eleventh of June last year. I can't remember exact times – it'll all be in the report of the inquest, of course – but after the service she went back to the vicarage, leaving him to put things straight, and to his prayers. When he didn't appear at lunchtime she went over to the church, and found him lying dead on the floor. The inquest verdict was death from natural causes. His heart had just stopped. After all, he was eighty-eight. It seems reasonable to deduce from what she said in court that she never saw the chalice again, and probably never gave it another thought until the Georgian plate was displayed in the Chapter House. She worshipped old Viney, and was completely bowled over. And, as I've told you, she was a very simple, limited person.'

Pollard sat deep in thought, absently running a hand through his hair. Toye searched briefly in the case file.

'There's the mention Miss Ridd made of a hiker, who came in during the service, sir, and went out again.'

'Was her eyesight reasonably good?' Pollard asked. 'I

mean, might she have mistaken a local inhabitant for a hiker?'

'I can only say that I didn't notice anything wrong with her sight at any time,' Eric Lacy replied.

Pollard went on to ask who would have assumed responsibility for the church building and its contents after Barnabas Viney's death, and learnt that Mrs Gillard would have done so as churchwarden.

'Mrs Gillard?' he said thoughtfully. 'And she stated in court that she had never seen the chalice Ethel Ridd was talking about, and knew nothing about it, didn't she? Well, assuming that Ethel Ridd really saw it that morning, it disappeared between the end of the service and the vicarage lunchtime, which certainly narrows things down, but unfortunately it's some time ago ... There's one other matter where you might be able to help us, Mr Archdeacon. Apart from Ethel Ridd and the reporter, did anyone leave the Consistory Court early? Before the lunch break, I mean? If the murderer decided to act because of her remarks about the chalice, he must have got going pretty quickly. She might, for instance, have decided to shut up the vicarage on her way home, to save going out again.'

Regretfully, Eric Lacy was of no assistance here. He had sat just forward of the front row of the public seats, and had noticed little or nothing of what went on further back. At his suggestion a telephone call was made to the cathedral's head verger, who came across the green from his house. Here there was definite help, but of a negative kind. No one, Pollard was assured, had left the Chapter House after the exit of Ethel Ridd and the reporter until the Chancellor had risen for lunch.

'The only other thing I can suggest,' Eric Lacy said, after the verger had been thanked and had departed, 'is that you ask Robert Hoyle, the Rector of Pyrford and Ambercombe, if he noticed anything at all worth mentioning about the general public present. He's an awfully sound nice chap.'

'I'll do that thing,' Pollard replied.

Soon afterwards he left with Toye, feeling that the interview had produced a number of points needing careful consideration. A soft drizzling rain was falling, through which the great towers of the cathedral reared up, dark and impassive. Strange to think, he meditated, that they were standing there looking exactly the same while Tadenham Abbey was being liquidated, and the funny business over the chalice being hatched.

As they drove back to Westbridge, they made a provisional timetable for the next morning.

'A look round the church first,' Pollard said, 'to get old Viney's death in focus ... Stop grinning, blast you. It's not an excuse to inspect the architecture. Then Mrs Gillard. I want to know how soon she got there, and if he had put things away after the service, or just left them on the altar, where anybody coming in could have picked up the chalice. And as we're up there, we'll drop in on this Sandford chap. List C, and Ridd's next door neighbour. All this hinges to some extent on what the forensic lab report is, of course.'

'I'm dead sure you're on a cert there, sir,' Toye said comfortably.

His optimism was justified. A report was waiting for them to the effect that the brick dust and fragments just tested were identical with the samples found under the copper in the scullery and in the wound in the deceased's head.

Cheered by this first definite progress Pollard rang his wife Jane at their home in Wimbledon. They talked discreetly in their usual code.

'I don't think the car I came to look at is quite such a write-off as I expected,' he told her. 'And while I'm down here I've decided that it's worth following up that second car I told you about.'

Jane expressed keen interest.

'Well, it looks as though the trip could turn out worthwhile after all,' she said. 'I suppose it means that you'll be away longer than you thought, though? Why, oh why didn't I marry a nine-to-five commuter, I wonder? Great doings here, by the way. Both the twins have been given parts in the nativity play their class is doing at the end of term. Andrew's to be the Archangel Gabriel, if you can believe it, and Rose the innkeeper's wife. I've been roped in as an auxiliary wardrobe mistress! ...'

*

Inspector Frost was inevitably chagrined on the following morning when confronted with the report from the forensic laboratory.

'My chaps ought to have spotted the stuff,' he said gloomily. 'And from the look of it we've wasted days over this bloody vagrant business.'

Pollard attempted consolation.

'We'd never have spotted it ourselves if the idea that the murder could have been a planned job hadn't suddenly hit us. And it isn't a conclusive proof of this, by any means. As to all you've done about checking up on strangers and where the locals were on Wednesday, it's giving us a flying start. Our next move is to work through your List C.'

After some further discussion it was agreed to keep the hunt for a vagrant going, but with reduced manpower, keeping alive the public impression that it was still on.

This matter having been settled, Pollard and Toye drove to Ambercombe and once more parked outside the church. Planks, an assortment of spades and a wheelbarrow close to Barnabas Viney's grave suggested that Ethel Ridd was to be buried beside the master she had served so devotedly.

'I'd forgotten about the funeral tomorrow for the moment,' Pollard said. 'We'd better turn up – one of us, anyway, and keep our eyes open. People have been known to give themselves away at funerals before now.'

He found the church interesting beyond expectation. There was nothing, he thought, looking around, that a comparatively small outlay for these inflationary days couldn't put right. A hardly altered little Norman building: it would be a crime to let it deteriorate further. Far better to part with a few pieces of Georgian plate ... Somebody was keeping the place spotless. Mrs Gillard, perhaps, now that Ethel Ridd was dead. He moved a few steps to admire an artistically lettered and framed list of vicars through the centuries, and wished Jane could see it, lettering being one of her things. Glancing back at the east window, it struck him that the bare branches of the trees made a fascinating geometrical pattern. He wandered round, studying the memorials and examining the carved pulpit and font cover.

Toye cleared his throat.

'This cupboard, sir. I reckon they keep the plate here, and the communion wine and wafers. Nice job. Decent bit of wood, and a good strong lock.'

Pollard came down to earth.

'Once again assuming that Ethel Ridd's chalice stuck with jewels really existed, I wonder if the old boy kept it in here with the rest of the stuff, and somebody managed to get a look inside and decided to lift the thing when there was an opportunity?'

They inspected the lock with the help of a torch and a lens, but it showed no sign of having been forced at any time, and no scratches suggesting the trying-out of keys.

'Could the opportunity have been when Viney collapsed and died?' Pollard mused. 'Rather suggestive, isn't it? Let's go and call on Mrs Gillard, and bring the conversation round to what exactly happened? Surely Ridd would have gone over to the farm for help.'

They went out into the porch. An elderly man in a frayed brown pullover was in the process of measuring out a grave with the help of a young lad. He gave the Yard pair an appraising stare and nodded briefly in response to Pollard's greeting.

'You'm Scotland Yard, I takes et?' he said. 'Turrible business, this yur murder upalong. I only 'opes yer gets 'ooever dunnet.'

'Yes, it is a terrible business,' Pollard agreed. 'I can only tell you we're all out on the job. You'll get a lot of people at the funeral tomorrow, I expect.'

''Sright. Strangers gawpin' an' tramplin' all over the churchyard. Newspapermen an' men from the telly, I shouldn't wonder. T'ain't seemly, to my mind, and 'er wouldn't of wanted 'em, pore maid. 'Er funeral's nobody's business but Ambercombe's.'

When they were safely out of earshot, Pollard remarked that some people would say that the chap had a parish pump outlook.

'But there's something to be said for living in a community,' he added.

Although a Londoner born and bred, Toye agreed.

At Ambercombe Barton a woman moving with brisk

purpose but looking tired and strained came to the door in response to their knock. She introduced herself as Margaret Gillard, and offered to send one of the men to find her husband.

'I don't think we need bring him away from his work at the moment, thank you,' Pollard replied. 'It's really you we want to see, Mrs Gillard, because of your connection with church affairs here ... What a marvellous kitchen, if I may say so,' he went on, looking around the huge stone-flagged room which yet managed to be both warm and cosy.

Margaret Gillard was gratified.

'The place is as old as the hills,' she told him. 'I don't know how many hundreds of years there've been Gillards here. We couldn't think of living anywhere else. The central heating's made all the difference, of course. It's oil-fired, and not a scrap of trouble, except when it comes to the oil bills these days. Would you care to come down to the other end?'

At the south end of the room a big modern window gave on to a fascinating patchwork of fields and woodland. A large sofa, comfortable chairs, a television set, budgerigars and a scatter of papers and magazines indicated the family's living area. Pollard accepted an offer of coffee.

When Margaret Gillard returned with it, he opened the conversation by asking her not to be irritated by further questions about the previous Wednesday.

'The fact is,' he told her, 'that people often forget things that they noticed at the time. I want you to think over your return home once again, if you will, from the time when you turned the corner into Pyrford. Did you notice anybody or anything in the least unusual?'

'I'll do that gladly,' she said, 'but I can't believe there was anything. I've thought and thought ...'

They had stopped in Pyrford to pick up the children, David and Rosemary, who came back from Westbridge Comprehensive on the school bus, getting in about half past four. She and her husband hadn't liked the idea of their coming home to an empty house, and had fixed for them to have tea with friends.

'And weren't we thankful we did, seeing what had hap-

64

pened to poor Ethel Ridd,' Margaret Gillard said with feeling.

'May I cut in here?' Pollard interrupted. 'I'm afraid I frightened your Rosemary yesterday evening. She was locking up the church, and I went rather quickly up the path to see if it was still light enough to see anything inside. I saw her back here afterwards, but I'm afraid she was a bit upset.'

To his surprise Margaret Gillard frowned and made a movement of irritation.

'What a funny girl she is: she never said a word to me when she came in. Talk to me about teenagers! She's been a real trial this last year. All nervy and shut up in herself. I often wish I'd had all boys. They aren't half the worry, for all the noise and mess they make, and tearing their clothes to rags.'

'Well, I do hope she soon got over the fright I gave her,' Pollard said. 'Sorry to interrupt you, Mrs Gillard. Do carry on.'

There was little more to tell. After chatting with their friends for a short time, she and her husband had driven home with the children, and she was certain that they had not met another car, nor passed anyone on foot. Everything had been as usual in the house.

'Mind you, I was dog tired after being in that stuffy Chapter House all day, and trying to follow what they were all saying, but I'm sure I'd have noticed anything out of the way,' she concluded.

Pollard had not expected to learn anything new, and began to steer the conversation towards Barnabas Viney's death.

'One of the things that makes this case difficult is the alternative ways of getting to the vicarage, and getting away again,' he said. 'I'd like your opinion on the possibilities, as you must know the lie of the land so well. Could we look at this large-scale map?'

They all moved to upright chairs at the big kitchen table, and Toye spread out the map. Margaret Gillard agreed that it was odd that a rough sort of man could have come up through Pyrford without being noticed.

'There's some people down there who seem to live at their windows,' she said. 'Of course he could have gone round behind Pyrford church and come up through the woods, or even come down along the top of the White-hallows. Hikers come that way in summer, but tramps, as we used to call them, never would. There's nothing to scrounge or steal up on the hills.'

Pollard seized on the operative word.

'Miss Ridd said something about a hiker looking in at the church on the morning Mr Viney died, didn't she? That would have been in June, of course.'

She gave him a quick look.

'Funny you should mention that. I'll remember it to my dying day. She'd found him lying on the floor in the church, and came running over here like a madwoman, saying that the hiker had come back and killed him. My husband had just come in to his dinner, and we dashed over expecting to find Mr Viney hurt and the place ransacked. It was all nonsense, of course, and after the inquest verdict was death from natural causes, she gave over talking so silly.'

'It must have been a dreadful shock to you,' Pollard said sympathetically. 'As churchwarden I expect you were afraid you'd find the plate gone.'

'I was, because with our Patronal coming along on June the twenty-fourth, Reverend Viney had been on at me to fetch the best plate from the bank in good time. You know how old people worry about things. So as I'd been into Westbridge the week before, I'd brought it back. While we were waiting for the ambulance I saw the key was in the lock of the cupboard where everything's kept, and looked inside, but the plate box was there and nothing was missing. I turned the key and brought it away.'

Nothing was missing ... except, perhaps, a medieval chalice of fantastic value, Pollard thought, watching Toye making a note of this important piece of information. *Had* the hiker come back, found the old man lying dead – or apparently dead, inspected the contents of the cupboard, and lifted the chalice just used in the service? But didn't that rule out the theory that the thief was Ethel Ridd's murderer, alert to the danger to himself of her unexpected

66

remarks in the Consistory Court? Surely only someone local would have reacted so promptly, and had the necessary knowledge of her movements and the local geography to carry out the murder so efficiently, and apparently without attracting a vestige of attention? A casual hiker hardly seemed to fit the bill.

Pollard was briefly tempted to comment on Ethel Ridd's reference in court to a missing chalice, but decided against it. If the thief were the murderer, the faintest rumour that the police were taking its existence seriously would almost certainly lead him to further drastic steps. Taking it out of the country, for instance. There was no evidence that Margaret Gillard lacked discretion, but she was certainly forthright in speech ... With sudden wry humour Pollard recognised that above all he wanted the Tadenham chalice to be a reality, and to recover it. Quite disgraceful for a CID man investigating a homicide, he told himself severely.

He asked a few more unnecessary questions to end the interview on a convincing note, and thanked Margaret Gillard for her help.

'I don't seem to have done much,' she said, escorting them to the door. 'We'll be thankful when the poor soul's safely in her grave tomorrow. It's getting me down being pestered by these reporters, and trying to fix for everything being done decent and proper ... There's Mr Sandford,' she added, as a battered MG shot past, heading for Pyrford. 'We'll be having another funeral one of these days the way he drives on these narrow roads.'

'Blast the man,' Pollard said, getting into the police car a few moments later. 'We've only missed him by about five minutes. We'd better take the Reverend Robert Hoyle next. He'll probably be trying to think of something to say at the funeral.'

Chapter 6

Robert Hoyle stood with his back to the fireplace in his study, frowning in concentration as he rammed tobacco into the bowl of a pipe with his thumb.

'No,' he said at last. 'I haven't the faintest recollection of anybody going out of the Chapter House after Ethel Ridd and the reporter left. But don't take it that nobody did, all the same. I was concentrating on the proceedings.'

He sat down, and glanced interrogatively at Pollard as he lit up, looking worried and rather distracted. His desk was littered with pieces of paper covered with jottings, but he had seemed to welcome the interruption of the Yard's visit.

'Have you been in touch with Archdeacon Lacy recently?' Pollard asked.

'About his idea that there could be something in what Ethel Ridd said about a jewelled chalice being used by Barnabas Viney on occasions? Yes. He rang me, and seemed tremendously excited. Church plate's his thing, of course.'

'What was your reaction?'

'Well,' Robert Hoyle hesitated briefly, and the vestige of a grin twitched the corners of his mouth, 'I had in decency to put up a show of interest, but frankly it strikes me as pretty far-fetched. I suppose I'm allergic to the subject of church plate at the moment. It's bedevilled me from the moment I accepted this living. You know all about the move to sell some of Ambercombe's, and the petition to the Consistory Court? I felt the whole business was humiliating: washing the parish's dirty linen in public. And now poor old Ethel Ridd's started another hare.'

'You think she imagined the existence of this chalice, then?' Pollard asked.

'Yes, I do. Both she and old Viney apparently lived in a sort of religious fantasy world of pre-Reformation days.'

'Where you can help us most, I think,' Pollard went on,

'is over Inspector Frost's List C. This is the list of local people who, purely on paper of course, could have killed Ethel Ridd. They were around during the vital period on Wednesday, November the nineteenth, and can't produce adequate supporting evidence of their alleged whereabouts. Can you tell us if any of them had known links with her?'

'Up to a point, that's an easy one,' Robert Hoyle replied, taking the list proferred by Toye. 'Naturally I can't speak of her contacts before I came here last March, but since then the short answer is that she virtually hadn't any locally. She was living the life of a recluse in the cottage old Viney left her, and only emerged to attend services at Ambercombe, do her caretaking job at the vicarage, and come down here once a week to draw her pension and do necessary shopping. She refused to speak either to me or my wife, although we made all the advances we could. You see, she saw me as representing the authority which had put an end to Ambercombe's separate identity as a parish. But I've never come across any serious hostility to her. She was looked on as a sort of comic eccentric.'

Pollard considered.

'Her chief contact seems to have been with your shop-cum-post office, then?'

To his surprise, there was a perceptible pause, and he thought he sensed deliberation.

'Yes. It's run by George Aldridge, my senior churchwarden, and his wife. George led the campaign to sell the Ambercombe plate, and so was in opposition to Ethel Ridd, who was one of the official objectors. But any idea that he murdered her on this score is fantastic, of course.'

'Why didn't Mr Aldridge stay in court for the whole hearing, sir?' Toye asked. 'You'd expect him to, being the senior churchwarden.'

Robert Hoyle glanced at him with interest.

'I see you're a church man, Inspector. It's a fair question. But we'd agreed beforehand that he should push off at lunchtime. His grocery supplier – Snip, it's called – delivers on Wednesday afternoons, and takes the next week's order and whatever, and it was important for him to get back to the shop. His wife copes with most of the post office work

69

but has nothing to do with the shop. I was in court all day myself, you see, and Mrs Gillard, the junior churchwarden, was there as well.'

'That seems to dispose of Mr Aldridge, then,' Pollard said, making a mental note to check up on the time taken over the delivery of the stock. 'I've got another copy of List C here. May we run through it, on the chance of a possible link with Ethel Ridd suggesting itself to you?'

He read out, with pauses between them, some dozen names, at each of which Robert Hoyle shook his head.

'Miss M. Rook, Laburnum Cottage, Pyrford?'

'Hold it,' Robert Hoyle said suddenly. 'I've never heard of any contact here, but if Ethel Ridd had one with anybody else down here or in Ambercombe, Martha Rook would hear about it. She's known locally as the News Chronicle. Heaven only knows how she gets on to things, but she does. Her cottage is opposite the shop.'

'Thanks,' Pollard said. 'We'll pay the lady a call. It's a type that's often worth cultivating. Next on the list is Mr W. Sandford, 3 Quarry Cottages, Ambercombe.'

'Bill Sandford. He's an interesting chap. Ex-rat race. Some relative left him a little money, and he opted out of a London job and came down here. He does part-time lecturing at the Westbridge College of Education to make ends meet, and otherwise goes his own way. He's an agnostic – or thinks he is – but we get on rather well. He's a compulsive coat-trailer, though, and used to bait poor Ethel Ridd, I'm afraid. But it's impossible to think of him killing her. Simply absurd.'

'Mr H. and Mrs M. Redshaw, The Old Rectory, Pyrford?'

'They're our village plutocrats. A literary pair. Of course you'll have come across his high-powered thrillers? Mrs Redshaw writes verses full of sweetness and light, which appear in lowbrow magazines for women and little booklets at Christmas. My wife came on a gem the other day, called *To a Water Vole*. It began "God's little water whimsy".'

'Not really?' Pollard ejaculated incredulously.

'Yes, really,' Robert Hoyle assured him with a broad grin. 'She gives little talks on the radio, too.'

70

Toye, looking puzzled, made a note that Mrs M. Redshaw wrote verses.

'This is abominable of me,' Robert Hoyle added. 'Both the Redshaws are most generous to the parish. It's just that we're on different wavelengths. You'll see what I mean. As to Ethel Ridd, Hugh Redshaw may have used her obvious eccentricities in one of his books, but I'm sure neither he nor his wife ever had any meaningful contact with her, to use that ghastly adjective.'

'You've aroused my curiosity,' Pollard told him. 'We've never interviewed literary types before, have we, Toye? I'll just finish off these names, and then we'll remove ourselves.'

Robert Hoyle had no further information to offer, however, and apologised for having given so little help.

'One never can tell what will turn out to be useful,' Pollard replied. 'You've been most patient, and I'm sorry to have taken up so much of your time when you've a lot in hand. We'll be along at the funeral tomorrow, if that's any comfort to you.'

After giving further reassurances, he left with Toye. They drove to a pub on the Westbridge road, and assessed the morning's work over sandwiches and beer in a corner of the bar, talking quietly, although there were few other patrons.

They agreed that both Margaret Gillard and Robert Hoyle gave the impression of being sound and straightforward.

'Both a bit lacking in imagination, perhaps?' Pollard added.

'Seeing that they both wrote the chalice right off?' Toye asked.

'Partly that. Their psychological make-up, too. As to the chalice having turned up, the morning's score is two–nil against, anyway. It makes the theory that the murderer stole it and felt obliged to shut Ethel Ridd's mouth for good less convincing, doesn't it? But we did get one or two bits of helpful gen from Hoyle about Ridd and the locals.'

After further discussion they decided to start off the afternoon's enquiries with a call on Martha Rook at Laburnum Cottage.

'If she's one of those who live at their windows, according to Mrs Gillard,' Pollard said, 'she may have seen Aldridge's return from Marchester on the afternoon of the murder, and what he did after the stock was delivered. By the way, did it strike you that Hoyle hung fire just a fraction when Aldridge was first mentioned?'

Toye had, but did not think it very significant. Rectors and their churchwardens pretty often didn't see eye to eye, and Reverend Hoyle probably wanted to be fair to the chap.

'Then there's this Sandford who lived next door to the deceased,' he went on, a note of disapproval in his voice. 'He doesn't sound all that stable to me. Work-shy, to start with. Now if there really was this chalice and somebody pinched it, on the face of it I'd say the job could be right up his street. Much more likely than that the writer couple were in on it.'

'Sandford's certainly one of our priorities,' Pollard agreed. 'I wonder where the hell he was off to this morning? Isn't there something in Frost's notes about the days he works at this college in Westbridge?'

Reference to the file established that Bill Sandford's working days were Mondays, Tuesdays and Fridays.

'He may have gone off anywhere today, then, seeing it's a Wednesday,' Pollard said. 'Perhaps Martha Rook, alias the News Chronicle, may be able to tell us if he's come back yet. But as we're in Pyrford, we may as well see the Aldridges after Rook. The Redshaws, and all the other people on List C who hadn't personal contacts with Ridd as far as the Rector knows, can wait.'

Ten minutes later they were on the road again, heading for Pyrford.

Martha Rook had a diminutive face with close-packed and slightly protuberant features. Her grey eyes were appraising behind steel-rimmed spectacles, and Pollard was instantly reminded of a small animal keenly alive to every development in its surroundings. He estimated her age as around seventy, and her circumstances as comfortable on a modest standard. According to the case file she had spent her entire working life in a grocery store at Westbridge, working her way up from a junior counter assistant to the cash desk. Her snug cottage faced the Village Stores and the Seven Stars across the green, and a Windsor armchair well supplied with cushions was strategically placed in the sitting-room window, so that she could also see all entrants to the village from the main road. A half-finished grey knitted stocking had been left on the chair when she got up to go to her front door.

'Well, I never,' she remarked briskly as she ushered Pollard and Toye into the room, and stooped to replace a draught excluder in the form of a grotesquely elongated velvet dachshund. 'Three policemen calling inside a week. That's a thing I never thought to come my way. Please to take a seat.'

She indicated a small settee by the fire, and switched on a lamp heavily encrusted with shells before sitting down facing her visitors on the other side of the hearth.

'Rector Hoyle sent you over, I'll be bound,' she added unequivocally.

'Quite right, Miss Rook,' Pollard replied, realising that finesse was not called for. 'You've got about the best view in the village of all the comings and goings, haven't you? We thought you might be able to help us, as you didn't go into Marchester on November the nineteenth.'

'No more I did.' Martha Rook's tone was regretful. 'A shocking cold I'd had, and the cough was still on me – a real noisy one. You've got to be a bit careful when you've topped your threescore and ten, and live on your own like I do.'

'So you were upstairs in bed?' Pollard asked in disappointment.

'Mercy on you, no! The day I take to my bed, I'll not be coming down again till they carry me feet first. I had a nice lie-in, true enough, but I was up and doing in time to wave off the coach party. All our outings start from outside the Stars, you see.'

'That's fine,' Pollard said. 'We know you've already told Inspector Frost that you didn't see any strangers about that day, but we'd like you to think back all the same. It's from

73

midday onwards that interests us. Of course, you weren't by the window all the time?'

Martha Rook clearly had no inhibitions on the subject of her observation post. By ten o'clock she had settled down with her knitting, and got a nice bit done that morning.

'Dead as a doornail the village was, with so many off to Marchester,' she told Pollard, 'until I'd had my dinner and cleared up, and gone back again with the one o'clock news switched on. Quarter past one the Marchester bus came in, and you could have knocked me down with a feather. There was Ethel Ridd, large as life! Nobody else: just her. Whatever could have happened for her to come away like that, I thought, seeing she'd been so hot against the Ambercombe plate being sold? I was so taken aback that I was a bit slow getting to the door and calling to her to come in and have a bite of something, and she went stalking up the road for dear life, pretending she hadn't heard. Then nothing else happened until the folk with cars started coming back.'

'I expect Mr Aldridge was the first,' Pollard hazarded. 'He had to leave the court early because of his weekly stores delivery, didn't he?'

'No, he wasn't,' Martha Rook replied with a slight sniff. 'The fuss there'd been, you'd think Pyrford Village Stores was one of those big London shops like Harrods. And he was nearly late for the Snip van, too, and I wonder he didn't meet with an accident, the reckless way he was driving to get here ahead of it, turning into the village as if he was on one of those motorways. I reckon he'd been round the Marchester wholesale depots after cheap fruit, and ran himself late. Turned the quarter to the hour it was.'

Toye remarked that it was wonderful how these big delivery vans managed to keep to schedule.

'That's right,' Martha Rook agreed. 'Wednesdays, three o'clock, and near as no matter except in the summer holiday season when the roads are choked up with visitors' cars. Last Wednesday the church clock had just struck the hour when it drew up. It has to park half on the green, being one of those long vehicles that never ought to be allowed, not in this country. The road over there would be blocked, else. But I'll say it's wonderful how quick they unload the stuff with that little platform going up and down, and those big trolleys.'

'It doesn't take long these days,' Toye said. 'I expect the van was soon off again?'

'Quarter to four, it went. Mind you, there are empties of one sort or another to take on, and Mrs Aldridge always has a cup of tea ready for the man. George Aldridge backed his own van into the yard, and slammed the doors shut right away. Very careful none of his stores get pinched, is George.'

'Who did get back first, Miss Rook?' Pollard asked, harking back to his original question.

'Mrs Redshaw, wife of the writer up at the Old Rectory. She was back about ten minutes before George Aldridge. She didn't go past here, of course, but turned up Church Lane to the house. Been doing a bit of shopping in Marchester, I daresay, getting some of those foreign things to eat that they're so fond of. My friend Mrs Tucker who works for her mornings says she wouldn't touch the stuff, not if you paid her. Mr Redshaw was later. He'd've been looking things up in the library at Marchester for his books. Just on five it was, when he turned in. She's got her own car: petrol's nothing to them. Writes poetry, she does. Very nice, some of it.'

When he could stem the flow Pollard managed to elicit the times of return of other residents who had come back from Marchester in their own cars.

'By the way,' he asked casually, 'did you happen to notice when Mr Sandford of Ambercombe came home?'

'He never,' Martha Rook replied categorically. 'Not Wednesday night. You can't miss that old rattleshaker of his going by. I reckon he was out on the tiles. I was on the listen for the coach, what's more, and when a lot of 'em crammed in here it was that hot I opened a bit of window. I'd've heard him, right enough, if he'd come back.'

In reply to further questions they learnt that Mrs Tucker and other cronies of Martha Rook's had hurried across to her cottage on disembarking from the coach at approximately six-thirty, and she had been regaled with a detailed account of the morning's astonishing events in the Chapter House.

'What did you make of this story of a jewelled chalice, Miss Rook?' Pollard asked, as soon as he could get a word in.

'A lot of rubbish,' she replied robustly. 'Living up there on her own, and missing old Mr Viney after being his housekeeper all those years, it's not surprising that she was getting fancies, poor soul.'

'I expect other people off the coach went in to tell Mr Aldridge how things had gone in court during the afternoon?' Pollard tried tentatively.

'Nobody'd stayed after the end of the morning. Dull as ditchwater it'd got after Ethel Ridd marched out, they all said. Anyway, the Stores shut at six o'clock sharp, and George Aldridge wouldn't have demeaned himself to come out and hear the news from all the rag, tag and bobtail. He'd reckon it was Rector's business to let him know, him being churchwarden.'

Rather reluctantly Pollard decided that it would be unwise to question her further at this stage on George Aldridge's movements after the departure of the Snip van at a quarter to four. In any case he could easily have slipped out in the gathering dusk, and returned later without her seeing him. There was no street lighting in the village.

'Could Aldridge have slipped out after he put his van away, and somehow made the trip to Ambercombe vicarage without his wife knowing?' he said, as they walked across the green five minutes later. 'Impossible, I should think, and the idea of them conspiring to murder Ridd seems a bit melodramatic. We'll go and have a look at them both though ... What's biting you?'

Toye had come to a halt beside a small blue van which bore the inscription PYRFORD VILLAGE STORES *G. M. Aldridge*, in bold white lettering.

'Nice little job,' he remarked. 'Get you here from Manchester in forty minutes, easy. You'd think that if getting back for his stock delivery mattered enough to contract out of the court hearing, that he wouldn't have run it so fine.'

'Oh, I don't know,' Pollard said. 'If he's the shrewd business man Martha Rook hinted, it could hang together all right. Tempting offers for boxes of apples and whatever at the wholesalers, and then getting caught up in a traffic jam. He seems to have got a flourishing little emporium from the look of it.'

They contemplated the display of groceries in the shop window, most of which carried labels indicating special offers, exceptional bargains and finest quality. A gay poster with a border of holly and robins advertising Christmas goods within recommended an early visit. Useful hardware in the shape of dustbins and gardening implements was grouped on the pavement. As Pollard opened the door the shrilling of an electric bell proclaimed their arrival. A dark man in a white coat who gave the impression of striking an attitude greeted them effusively from behind the counter.

'Only this morning I was saying to Rector that we'd be seeing you gentlemen about the parish again today, and it's a comfort to every man and woman in the place to know Scotland Yard's here to clear up this dreadful business. And if there's anything in the world either Mrs Aldridge or I can do to be of service to you, gentlemen, you've only to say the word, and that's a fact.'

'Thank you,' Pollard replied. 'At the moment we're just making a routine check on information already received. May we have a word with you in private, if it's convenient?'

'Certainly, sir, if you'd kindly step this way.' George Aldridge raised a counter flap, emerged and lowered it again with an economy of movement born of long practice. 'My office is out at the back. We shan't be disturbed. My wife'll take over, won't you, dear? Not that it's a busy time, early afternoon midweek. Not at this time of year, that is.'

Pollard's good afternoon was echoed by the woman behind the grille of the post office section of the counter, but he noticed that she barely raised her eyes from a form she was filling in as he passed. The office to which he and Toye were conducted was uncomfortably cramped, and fitted up to an extent which struck him as high-powered for so modest a business. With some difficulty they manoeuvred themselves on to the two chairs facing George Aldridge

77

across his flat-topped desk. The latter had already embarked on an unsolicited account of Ethel Ridd's shopping habits. Letting it flow unchecked, Pollard studied the man's pale face, black boot-button eyes and faintly ridiculous little waxed moustache. Then, by a trick of the light, he caught sight of the beads of sweat standing out on the forehead.

'When one realises what a secluded life Miss Ridd led,' he said when a pause presented itself, 'obviously you and Mrs Aldridge must have known her better than most people. Were you surprised at her behaviour at the Consistory Court?'

Obviously gratified by this acknowledgment, George Aldridge combined a shrug with an expansive movement of his hands.

'In a manner of speaking, sir, I was and I wasn't, if you get me. With all her funny ways I'd have thought she'd have had more sense of what was proper than to create like that in a court of law. But let's face it, she and old Mr Viney weren't – well, like other people, living in the past the way they did. Between you and me it was shameful the way things were let go up there, parish and church alike. Why the Archdeacon didn't take steps, I'll never understand. And now here we are in Pyrford with Ambercombe tacked on to us, and the church half falling down, and still not free to sell plate there's not a scrap of use for with only a handful of people ever stepping inside the church door. Nice job we're landed with, Mr Hoyle and me.'

'We know that Miss Ridd returned here on November the nineteenth by a bus from Marchester getting in at a quarter past one,' Pollard said, abruptly transposing the conversation into a more official key. 'The Chancellor rose for the lunch break at one o'clock, I understood, but even so she would, of course, have arrived back here before you?'

There was a perceptible pause and change of atmosphere.

'Oh, yes, of course,' George Aldridge replied, his speech gathering momentum. 'She'd have been up the hill and back home quite a time before me, you see. I took the opportunity of calling at a fruit and vegetable wholesalers in Marchester. Petrol being what it is, you've got to make full use of any trip you make these days. I can't have got away from

78

Marchester much before two. Dreadful, the traffic blocks in the middle of the town. It gets worse and worse, and the City Council ...'

'What time did you get back here, Mr Aldridge?' Pollard cut in.

'Soon after the half-hour, to the best of my recollection.'

'Got that, Inspector?' Pollard asked Toye, without particular emphasis. 'And you didn't, as you've already told Inspector Frost, see any stranger around from then on?'

'Not a sign of one. Mind you, what with the Snip delivery van arriving, and checking the stuff and getting the store straight again, I can't say I had much time for what was going on outside. I was on the go right up to six when we closed, and after that backwards and forwards to the store filling up gaps on the shelves, and then there was the paperwork in here. We never sat down to our meal till gone half past six,' George Aldridge concluded breathlessly, taking out a handkerchief and refraining in the nick of time from mopping his brow. He blew his nose vigorously.

'Well, I think that covers the ground,' Pollard said, reverting to a more conversational tone. 'Thank you for your help, Mr Aldridge. Now, just before we go, we'd like a word with your wife to round off the record, if you'd take over in the shop. Ask Mrs Aldridge to join us, would you, Inspector?'

Toye was already opening the office door. Taken aback by the swiftness of the manoeuvre, George Aldridge found himself being politely but firmly ushered out. A few moments later Toye showed in a short, rather plump woman. She was curiously colourless, with her pale skin, pale yellow hair and spectacles with transparent frames.

Her replies to Pollard's questions were equally colourless, incorporating his own words ... Yes, she had been in charge of the shop on November the nineteenth ... No, she had not seen any strangers about ... Yes, her husband had returned in the early afternoon because of the stock being delivered.

'What time did he get back?' Pollard asked.

'I didn't notice to the minute. I'd opened up again after the dinner hour.'

'What time is your dinner hour?'

'One to two-fifteen.'

'What did he do after the delivery van had gone?'

'After the delivery van had gone? There's all the stuff to check.'

'Did he go out again that day?' Pollard insisted, repressing an urge to seize Mabel Aldridge and shake her.

'No, he didn't go out again.'

'Just like a cat,' Pollard remarked, walking with Toye to the car five minutes later.

'Cat, sir?' Toye stared at him. 'Ventriloquist's dummy, I'd call her.'

'She's got a cat's utter non-involvement. Look how different they are in the home from dogs. Let's go up to Ambercombe. I feel we're under observation on both flanks.'

They drove up the long hill, already becoming familiar, past the Barton and on to the church gate where Toye pulled off the road. They sat in silence for some moments.

'Let's have the map out,' Pollard said. 'Could Aldridge possibly have got back here from Marchester before Ridd, somehow known that she would call in at the vicarage, killed her, and got home in time to take the goods delivery? Never mind for the moment what possible motive he might have had. He would have had to come along this minor farm road from the east side of these hills. I'm certain Martha Rook parked in her window would have spotted him if he'd gone up through Pyrford, and she saw him drive in from the main road.'

They spread out the ordnance sheet on the steering wheel and pored over it.

'No,' Toye said at last. 'It simply isn't on. Even if Aldridge had managed to park near the cathedral, and had belted out of the Chapter House, he'd still have to get clear of the city with all the lunchtime traffic. Add to that the fact that the road from Marchester running west and round the north of the Whitehallows is slow. Look how it detours through villages. You couldn't get up any real speed on it. Then this side road branching off it and coming through Ambercombe here isn't much more than a lane, as Mrs Gillard said. He couldn't have made it before two o'clock

– if then, even if he'd come straight from the court.'

'And if Ridd was stalking through Pyrford for dear life just after one-fifteen, she'd have been up here easily by a quarter to two,' Pollard said thoughtfully. 'Why did Aldridge lie to make out that he got back to Pyrford earlier than he did, though? Funny business of some sort, but what? Probably not our pigeon, but I'd like to make sure. I'll ring the Super at Marchester from the kiosk along there, and ask if they could check up with possible wholesalers.'

The call having been made, they turned up the lane to Quarry Cottages, Toye remarking that it was an improvement on the evening before, anyway. Pollard agreed. The blanket of low cloud had vanished, and the sky was a clear turquoise overhead, merging into pure gold in the south-west. The Whitehallows, touched here and there by the last rays of the setting sun, were no longer menacing but majestic. He sniffed the cold sharp air with enjoyment.

As they had half expected, there was no sign of life in Bill Sandford's cottage, or his car in the open shed where he apparently kept it. Pollard wrote a brief note on one of his official cards to the effect that he would call immediately after Miss Ridd's funeral the next morning. If Mr Sandford was unable to be available at this time, would he please ring the Westbridge police station? Pollard added the telephone number, and dropped the card through the letter box.

They went back to the car. As Toye switched on the lights the noise of a heavy vehicle grinding up the hill from Pyrford became audible.

'Tractor?' he queried.

'Getting quite the little countryman, aren't you?' Pollard remarked.

A moment later a school bus appeared, and drew up a short distance away. It was apparently the end of the run, as only half a dozen children tumbled out with bags and satchels swinging from their shoulders. The boys, with keen interest, instantly surrounded the Hillman. Pollard's attention, however, was focused on Rosemary Gillard. The last to leave the bus, she came down the steps chatting with another girl. Suddenly she saw the police car, froze for an instant, and with terror in her face turned and fled in the direction of the Barton, her astonished companion staring after her.

Pollard turned to Toye.

'There's something a damn sight more than adolescence wrong with that kid,' he said.

Chapter 7

Pending further developments in the investigation of Ethel Ridd's murder, the *Westbridge Evening News* was publishing a series of special articles to keep alive its readers' interest. On their return to the police station Pollard and Toye found a copy of the current issue in their temporary office. It featured Barnabas Viney, whose striking face looked out from under the caption THE LONG INNINGS.

It was the same photograph that the Archdeacon had shown them. Pollard scrutinised it again, subsiding slowly onto a chair as he did so. The body worn almost transparent, he thought, and the spirit or whatever positively blazing through it ... Utterly uncompromising ...

The telephone on the table bleeped suddenly. Toye lifted the receiver.

'Marchester,' he told Pollard, handing it over.

Pollard introduced himself, exchanged greetings with Superintendent Bosworth of Marchester, and listened at some length. It appeared that there had been no difficulty in picking up George Aldridge's trail after he left the Consistory Court at one o'clock on Wednesday 19 November. He had arrived in his van at Bablake & Harroway's wholesale fruit depot just before one-fifteen. The salesman who dealt with him was due to go off to dinner at half past one, and had his eye on the time. Aldridge had bought a crate of apples and another of oranges, and the salesman had remarked that the chap had been in one hell of a hurry, and driven off like a bomb when they'd loaded the stuff into the van. He was well away by the half-hour. There were two other possible wholesale warehouses in Marchester, but enquiries had shown that Aldridge had not visited either of them that day.

'Like us to find out if he called in anywhere else?' Superintendent Bosworth asked.

'We'd be grateful if you'd discover which road he took out

of the town,' Pollard replied. 'He was up to something fishy, but at the moment it doesn't look like tying up with our show. Still, we'd better make sure.'

After a further brief conversation and renewed thanks for Marchester's prompt help he rang off, and passed on the information to Toye.

'So exit George Aldridge, I take it?' he concluded.

Toye, who had listened impassively, nodded his assent.

'He's right out as far as Ridd goes, whatever he was up to. If he didn't leave the wholesale place until just on half past one, he couldn't possibly have made Ambercombe in time to kill her and get back to Pyrford by a quarter to three on that road going north of the Whitehallows. It's a long way round.'

Pollard sat absently drumming on the table with the fingers of his right hand.

'Let's go and eat,' he said suddenly. 'It's a long time since that bar snack.'

The dining room of their hotel produced an unexpectedly good meal. Pollard worked through it rather abstactedly, while Toye perused the *Westbridge Evening News*. Over Stilton and water biscuits Pollard asked if there were anything decent on the box.

'There's a Western,' Toye admitted guardedly. '*Black Gulch Deadline*. Dod Buffelsfontein and Dimity Rose.'

Pollard grinned.

'It's all yours. Go and give what passes for your brain a break. I feel like doing a Garbo.'

The rapport existing between them was such that Toye accepted the proposed programme without comment beyond remarking that the TV room was on the first floor. He gulped down his coffee and departed. Pollard sat on at their table for a few moments appreciatively watching his decorous progress to the door. Then he gathered up the case file and the newspaper, and went to ring Jane before settling down to some hard thinking. Later, feeling relaxed as a result of a brief escape into his personal world, he located a quiet corner in the less frequented of the hotel's two lounges, ordered more coffee, and installed himself in a comfortable chair.

The coffee arrived and was hot and good. He sat sipping it, letting his thoughts range freely over the events of the past two days. Presently he began to co-ordinate them. The one indisputable basic fact was that Ethel Ridd's murder had been premeditated, and had taken place in Ambercombe vicarage in the afternoon or early evening of Wednesday 19 November.

In an odd way the day and the hour seemed to reverberate in his mind. If there had been premeditation on the killer's part, why did he choose that particular day? Was it because it had been known well in advance that an unusual number of people would be absent from Ambercombe and Pyrford because of the Consistory Court hearing in Marchester? This would cut both ways, though. If he was a local man – and Ethel Ridd's fantastically restricted social contacts and his knowledge of her habits made this almost certain – the fact that he was around, and not in Marchester himself, was bound to come to the knowledge of the police. From the standpoint of an alibi it seemed a risky day to choose. The alternative explanation could only be that he had no choice: that something had happened earlier in the day making it imperative for him to murder Ethel Ridd at once. And in default of a shred of evidence in another direction, this pointed to her outburst in court about the allegedly missing chalice, and so to the theory that the thing really did exist, and that the murderer had found this out and stolen it, on or after the day of Barnabas Viney's death. And that he could have been involved in the latter...

One step at a time, Pollard thought. If only we could get definite proof that there really was a chalice. He opened the file and turned once more to the report of the events in the Consistory Court. What exactly had Ethel Ridd said? ' 'Tisn't the ordinary one I'm talking about. It's the little one Father Viney'd use in and out for Saints' days. It had jewels stuck in it.'

He read her words several times before being suddenly struck by the phrase 'in and out'. Wasn't this rather odd? Wouldn't old Viney, with his obsession with Ambercombe's link with Tadenham Abbey, have used a medieval chalice that he'd discovered on every suitable occasion? Not on

Sundays or for any service at which a local congregation might turn up and discover his secret, but as Ethel Ridd had said in evidence, nobody from the village came to church on weekdays, barring herself. So why did the old man – according to her – only use this particular chalice 'in and out'?

Finding no answer to this question Pollard began to wonder where Barnabas Viney might have hidden away a chalice. Ethel Ridd couldn't have known, or she would have told the court where it had been kept as additional confirmation of her story. The more Pollard thought about this point, the more curious he found it. A woman who did the housework or generally kept the household ticking over always seemed to know where everything was. At any rate Jane's omniscience in this sphere was a joke in his own home, and his mother had been just the same. Of course Ridd didn't seem to have been awfully bright, and Viney was obviously a cautious old chap. Archdeacon Lacy had said that Ambercombe's Georgian plate wasn't all that valuable, but it had been kept in the bank, and had always been taken back there after being got out for festivals ...

Pollard made an abrupt movement, almost knocking over the coffee tray in his excitement. If there was a chalice, this is what the old boy did with it, he thought. I swear it ties up. The Gillard woman said Viney made a thing of getting the stuff out of the bank well before it was needed. She mentioned a plate box, too. He'd have kept everything locked up in that cupboard at the back of the church for the short periods involved, but was too security-minded to risk a real treasure there permanently.

His mind began to race ahead but was brought up short by a theological query. Were there Saints' days close to Christmas and Easter and Ambercombe's Patronal festival on 24 June? The Feast of Stephen, of course, on Boxing Day, when old Wenceslas looked out ...

The next moment he was crossing the lounge *en route* for the television room. This was the sort of thing a church man like Toye would know. He opened the door cautiously and peered in. Clearly the deadline had arrived in Black Gulch. Dimity Rose in an immaculate late Victorian print frock, and without a single braided flaxen curl out of place,

86

was lashed to a tree trunk in the direct line of fire between a gang of desperadoes and an agonised Dod Buffelsfontein, all of whose supporters had already been picked off. However, a posse of unmistakable Sheriff's men was just entering the mouth of the Gulch with the obvious intention of assailing the gang from the rear ...

Regardless of protests from indignant viewers, Pollard made his way over to Toye in the front row.

'Come on out of it,' he hissed into his ear.

Back in the lounge, a surprised Toye produced the required information about Saints' days without hesitation.

'There's St Thomas the Apostle on December the twenty-first,' he said. 'St Stephen, December the twenty-sixth; St John the Evangelist, December the twenty-seventh; and Holy Innocents, December the twenty-eighth. Then some people would call January the first –'

'That'll do for Christmas,' Pollard cut in. 'What about Easter?'

'Well, there you've got a moveable feast, of course. The Annunciation's March the twenty-fifth, and at the other end St Mark is April the twenty-fifth, and St Philip and St James, May the first. Either side of St John the Baptist, there's Barnabas on June the eleventh, and St Peter on June the twenty-ninth.'

Pollard stared at him.

'My God, you know your stuff! Why didn't you go into the Church?'

Toye admited coyly that he had given it serious thought, but the long training had put him off.

'I might have a bash at becoming a Lay Reader when I retire,' he added. 'What's all this in aid of, by the way?'

Pollard told him. For a full minute the pair sat in silence.

'Aren't plate boxes often lined with velvet or whatever?' Pollard asked suddenly.

'That's right,' Toye replied. 'If something extra had been fitted in, there could be marks. The forensic chaps might be able to get on to it.'

'The bank'll dig its toes in about letting us have the thing.'

Toye suggested getting an authorisation from Mr Hoyle.

'Good idea. We can catch him after the funeral tomorrow morning: it's too late to do anything about it tonight, and the poor chap's all steamed up, anyway. We'll come back to Westbridge and go to the bank after we've seen Sandford.'

'Nice handy base, that chap's cottage, for spotting anything valuable in the Church, and for lifting it, come to that,' Toye commented.

'My own thoughts entirely,' Pollard replied. 'Let's pack it in, shall we?'

Robert Hoyle in surplice and stole stood at the gate of Ambercombe churchyard to receive Ethel Ridd's coffin. The hearse moved off through a gap in the crowd of onlookers cleared by the police. When it had passed people closed in again, forming a solid encircling wall of humanity. Under a flat grey sky the air was perfectly still and the crowd silent, only an occasional cough or shuffle of feet indicating its presence. Intermittently an autumn leaf fluttered to the ground by a devious route. Robert Hoyle's voice, unemotionally confident, dominated the gathering ...

'Neither death, nor life ... nor things present, nor things to come ... nor any other creature' – he paused almost imperceptibly – 'shall be able to separate us from the love of God ...'

Pollard, standing with Toye in the place reserved for them by Inspector Frost beyond the porch, watched the pathetically small cortège advance. Because of the tiny capacity of the church he had chosen to observe the proceedings in the churchyard. Robert Hoyle led the way inside, followed by the coffin on a wheeled bier propelled by the undertaker's men. It was heaped with wreaths and simple bunches of garden flowers. Whatever the villagers' attitude to Ethel Ridd had been during her lifetime, they were now expressing their solidarity with her in her death. Probably mixed motives, some of them unconscious, Pollard thought. A community's instinctive hostility against the killer of one of their number, a propitiatory gesture occasioned by a sense of guilt, and a drawing together in the face of the ultimate invincible enemy. In the absence of any kindred of the dead woman, Margaret Gillard and a man who was presumably her husband followed the coffin as chief mourners. Pollard studied Matthew Gillard with interest. A sturdy figure, with an obstinate sensible face tanned by sun and wind, he looked straight ahead with the deadpan expression of a man carrying out an unavoidable duty under conditions of intolerable publicity.

During the interval which followed Pollard ran his eye over the crowd. He identified the Aldridges, and got the impression that George, at least, was carefully avoiding his glance. In general people's faces were expressionless as they stood close together, muffled up against the cold. At intervals they moved their feet in the chilling damp grass. Press and television photographers in black jackets and hung about with their gear moved about restlessly, irrelevant as insects. Pollard, beginning to feel cold himself, hunched his shoulders and shifted his weight from one foot to another as he looked around. A few yards away a spider's web linked one arm of the granite cross over Barnabas Viney's grave with its shaft, and was spangled with bright drops of moisture. Some of the graves were carefully tended and defiantly bright with the rich glowing colours of dahlias and chrysanthemums. Others were merely indicated by stunted and heeling headstones, pointers to wholly forgotten generations. A stark mound of damp earth and an open trench lined with greenery awaited the mortal remains of Ethel Ridd.

At long last the massive oak door of the church opened protestingly, and a ripple of heightened awareness passed over the waiting crowd.

The committal was quickly over. Margaret Gillard with compressed lips and a resolute expression scattered earth on the lowered coffin. Robert Hoyle pronounced the final grace, and out of the corner of his eye Pollard saw Inspector Frost's attention automatically switch over to the immediate problem of traffic dispersal.

For a time Robert Hoyle stood talking with groups of his parishioners. When he finally went back into the church Pollard and Toye followed. They found him extricating himself from his surplice, and listened to his wholehearted expressions of gratitude to the police for their handling of sightseers and photographers at the funeral.

'I was simply dreading this morning,' he said, taking off his stole, 'but it all went so smoothly. I only wish your troubles were over, too. Can I do anything?'

Pollard put his request for an authorisation to remove the Ambercombe plate box and its contents from the bank.

'There'll be proper security, of course, and I'll give you an official receipt. I know you'll understand that I can't be explicit about why we want a look at it.'

'Of course,' Robert Hoyle replied. 'I'll let you have one right away if you can come down to the Rectory.'

Pollard explained that they had a date with Mr Sandford of Quarry Cottages, and it was arranged that they should pick up the authorisation later that morning. As they went down the churchyard path and out into the road, little knots of people still lingering and chatting eyed them curiously. They turned left, and then left again into the lane leading to the vicarage gate and Quarry Cottages. In answer to their knock the door of number 3 was opened by a man in an old coat over pyjamas. He was unshaven, with unkempt dark hair and bright blue eyes.

'Bill Sandford,' he stated briefly. 'The fuzz, I take it?'

Pollard introduced himself and Toye, and held out his official card.

'Not to worry.' Bill Sandford waved it away airily. 'It's so seldom that we get bogus coppers round here that I'll chance it. Come inside if you want to see me, and make yourselves at home. Excuse my *déshabille*, won't you? I don't go to work on Thursdays.'

Pollard recognised the compulsive coat trailing mentioned by Robert Hoyle, this time in regard to non-attendance at Ethel Ridd's funeral. Moreover there was an almost exaggerated contrast between Bill Sandford's personal appearance and the orderly and comfortable living room of the cottage. As Pollard sat down he registered clean whitewashed walls with original watercolours and interesting brass rubbings. There were rugs on the stone floor, well-filled bookcases and a table in the window with the tools of the calligrapher's trade neatly set out. A half-finished manuscript was fastened to a drawing board propped at an angle of about sixty degrees. It linked up in Pollard's mind with the framed list of the vicars of Ambercombe that he had noticed in the church. He sat down by the fire, facing Bill Sandford who dropped into a chair on the other side of the hearth.

'You knew the late Mr Viney fairly well, didn't you, Mr Sandford?' he opened.

Bill Sandford flung himself back, crossing his legs and surveying Pollard quizzically, who instantly sensed confidence behind the half-mocking stare ... This chap didn't kill Ridd, he thought instantly, but he's up to the neck in something phoney. Hell! Not another Aldridge situation, for heaven's sake ...

'I've no idea what degree of intimacy you imply by "fairly well",' Bill Sandford was countering.

'Casual visiting terms?' Pollard suggested, deciding to give the impression of allowing himself to be led down a tortuous garden path.

'If you like. I blew in now and again. I'm not a church goer.'

'Did he ever mention the chalice Miss Ridd claimed that he sometimes used?'

Bill Sandford assumed an expression of mock astonishment.

'Don't tell me that an eminent CID Super has fallen for poor old Ridd's yarn!'

'I've no intention of telling you anything, Mr Sandford. I'm here to ask questions, not to give information.'

'The answer,' Bill Sandford replied with a bow, 'is in the negative.'

'Did Miss Ridd herself ever mention this chalice to you?'

This time there was a shout of laughter.

'God, no! I was beyond the pale with our Ethel. An unbeliever, a pub crawler, and a chap given to suggestive overnight absences. Not a bloke you'd discuss the sacred vessels with. The first I ever heard of the thing was when she lobbed her blockbuster at the Chancellor in court.'

'Presumably, though, you were not beyond the pale with Mr Viney,' Pollard observed.

'True. Simply, I deduced, because I read history at Oxford and had heard of Bernard of Clairvaux and the Cistercians.

91

Tadenham Abbey was a Cistercian foundation, and Amber-combe church one of its outposts. They owned all the land round here till Henry VIII weighed in. Of course, you've heard all about Barny's obsession?'

'Could he be considered mentally normal?'

Bill Sandford shrugged, and sat dangling a slipper from a bare foot.

'Can you? Can I? What's your yardstick? He certainly wasn't certifiable. His obsession with the past and the Cistercian way of life got him the reputation of being a bit nor-nor-west, but in other directions he carried on normally. There were always the basic church services, even if practically nobody turned up, and the Church Council or whatever it's called was more or less moribund. Over the last few years he got too frail to visit people, but they could always come along and get things signed or whatever. I found him interesting, actually, provided I took his obsession as read. He read *The Times* from the standpoint of somebody in Mars, which was intriguing. Now and again I did an odd job for him in Westbridge after he couldn't get his driving licence renewed. Cashing a cheque or buying a book. Things beyond the scope of our Ethel.'

'How did she fit into the picture?'

'She accepted the situation uncritically. Her IQ was low, and anything in the way of abstract or logical thinking was beyond her, as far as I could judge. She functioned more or less as an automaton. After the parishes were amalgamated she evolved another routine of domestic chores and cleaning the church, and so on. Haven't I read somewhere that if you cut off a hen's head it still goes on running in circles?'

Pollard declined the gambit.

'You were her next door neighbour. To your personal knowledge was she ever visited by a stranger?'

'Never. Her social life was virtually nil, apart from an occasional visit from a local do-gooder. She refused to let either of the Hoyles into the cottage. In her eyes he was a usurper.'

While keeping the conversation going Pollard was coming to a decision on tactics. By now he was convinced that Bill Sandford had a genuine alibi for the time of Ethel Ridd's murder, and that he was keenly looking forward to producing it out of a hat at the end of a lengthy and time-consuming period of questioning. He was equally sure in his own mind, however, that beneath the confidence of being able to blow a murder charge sky-high there was wariness towards the police on some other – and possibly related – issue. He decided to chance his hand.

'Well, thanks for your filling-in, Mr Sandford,' he said. 'Now, may we have your alibi for the afternoon and evening of November the nineteenth?'

The astonishment and deflation in Bill Sandford's face was so reminiscent of his son Andrew's reactions to anticipation of a try-on that Pollard suppressed a grin with difficulty. It was only a fleeting expression, however.

'Sure, Superintendent. Didn't Swinburne or somebody say that even the weariest river winds somewhere safe to sea? Now, let me think ... On leaving the Chapter House, I proceeded – there's a real one hundred per cent fuzz-word for you – to the Dean Street car park, got into my car, and drove to Westbridge. I got there at a quarter to two, just in time for a pint and a meat pie at the Man-o'-War, my favourite pub. It's down by the docks, and its patrons are a super crowd: even my vocabulary's been enlarged since I took to going there. After the landlord booted us out I drove to my current girlfriend's flat, 17b Wentworth Road. She was at work, but I have a latchkey. Time of arrival: about 2.25 p.m. Witness: Mrs Trevor-Montley, widow, who observed it as usual from behind the net curtains of her ground-floor flat, number 17a. My girlfriend is Miss Angela Barrow, employed as a secretary by Mr Tomkinson, senior partner of Messrs Tomkinson, Heriot and Tomkinson, Solicitors, of Portway, Westbridge. She returned home at approximately 5.15 p.m., and we spent an enjoyable evening and night in each other's company. On the following morning we left together, Angela to her job, and I to come back here and get on with that illuminated address over there. I do a bit of calligraphy to help out. The first I heard about poor old Ethel was when I got back from work on Friday afternoon, and it seemed a good idea to clear out again at once.

93

Angela's firm is a bit Establishment, and I wanted time to think.'

'Got all the relevant facts, Inspector?' Pollard asked Toye without comment.

'Yes, sir.'

'Right. Well, I think that's all for the moment, Mr Sandford, thank you.'

He got up to go, but paused at the table.

'Nice job,' he commented. 'Did you do that list of Ambercombe vicars in the church?'

'Yea.' Bill Sandford sounded surprised. 'Kids' stuff, that: just plain. This sort of thing's a lot dicier, especially the gold leaf on the Roman capitals.'

At the door Pollard looked back, and met a pair of humorous but wary blue eyes.

'Shall we say honours easy, Mr Sandford?' he asked.

Out of earshot Toye snorted in disapproval.

'Wasting the time of the police like that! It's an offence. He's up to the neck in something all right. It sticks out a mile.'

'Your metaphors are a bit mixed, but I absolutely agree,' Pollard replied. 'As you imply, he's doing an Aldridge on us.'

'How many more dead ends are we going to land up in?' Toye demanded rhetorically. 'What about the List C people we haven't got round to yet?'

'My remark about the case being two jobs for the price of one seems to have been an underestimate,' Pollard agreed. 'Nothing for it but slogging on, though. We'll collect the chit from the Rectory, and then head for Westbridge. Check Sandford's alibi which will be perfectly sound, and then get that plate box from the bank.'

Chapter 8

'My position is simply intolerable, Superintendent,' Mrs Trevor-Montley assured Pollard, her full cheeks quivering with impotent indignation. 'After my husband died – he was a consultant at one of our leading hospitals before he retired – this house was too big for me. I wanted to stay in my old home with all its happy memories, so I sold the first floor to a man called Blount, for conversion into a flat, and kept the ground floor as a flat for myself, with the dear garden. Blount undertook to make the sort of flat that would attract really nice people, but he turned out to be completely unreliable. He made two cheap little flats and let them to people that one has absolutely nothing in common with. As far as the Hutchinsons go, I might be a great deal worse off: they're a quite inoffensive retired couple from somewhere in the Midlands, I believe. But the Barrow girl is a very different matter. Blount is absolutely unco-operative in the matter, and my solicitor tells me that I can get no redress from the law, unbelievable though it seems.'

The room was overheated, and crowded with furniture, china and silver. Pollard controlled his irritation with difficulty. He was convinced of the genuineness of Bill Sandford's alibi, and it was maddening to have to listen to this querulous verbiage for the sake of getting unnecessary confirmation for the record.

'You're referring, I take it, to the man who visits Miss Barrow here?' he prompted.

Mrs Trevor-Montley sighed heavily, and made a despairing gesture with pudgy hands.

'I am. I have spoken to her as if she were my daughter, reasoned with her, and finally suggested that her conduct is most unsuitable in a house in a good residential district like this. On every occasion she has been coolly insolent. Yes, coolly insolent,' Mrs Trevor-Montley repeated, as if savouring the phrase with satisfaction. 'She informed me that she had no intention of leaving her flat, and that her way of life was her affair and not mine. And to think that she is secretary to one of the partners in a very reputable firm of solicitors. I asked my own solicitor if it were not my duty to warn them about Miss Barrow's morals, but he advised against it.'

'That was sound advice,' Pollard told her. 'The laws of slander and libel are very dicey, you know. I wonder now, Mrs Trevor-Montley, if you can help us by thinking back to the afternoon of Wednesday, November the nineteenth. Last Wednesday week.'

'As it happens I remember it very well. The behaviour of that pair upstairs was particularly outrageous. I was just getting up from my afternoon rest at about half past two when the man arrived in his noisy dilapidated car, and parked it immediately outside. He then played a flourish on the horn. This was simply to annoy me, as he knew perfectly well that Miss Barrow would not have come home at that hour.'

'Did he go up to her flat?'

'He did. I happened to glance out of the window and saw him come in. A few moments later her front door slammed and he began to tramp about overhead. He has a key. As I said just now, it is a disgraceful situation.'

'Did he leave the flat in the course of the afternoon?'

'He did not. At intervals he made a lot of unnecessary noise overhead. Friends who were having tea with me remarked how inconsiderate he was. And after Miss Barrow came back at about a quarter past five the noise was even worse, and went on at intervals all through the evening, with a record player going as well. The man left the flat – with Miss Barrow – at twenty minutes to nine on the following morning.'

Having delivered this final piece of information in a portentous tone, Mrs Trevor-Montley compressed her lips and sat with closed eyes. Pollard risked a wink at Toye.

'Well, Mrs Trevor-Montley,' he said, 'your detailed information has been helpful. It's possible that we may want you to sign a written version of what you have told us, but I don't think it will be necessary.'

'The very last thing I want is to be mixed up in police proceedings. It would be most distasteful.' She stared at him with wide-open and resentful eyes.

'Actually,' Pollard told her, 'your evidence has saved you from being mixed up in some really sensational publicity. It has cleared Miss Barrow's visitor of all possibility of being involved in the Ambercombe murder.'

Mrs Trevor-Montley uttered a small scream, but rallied quickly.

'It wouldn't have surprised me in the least if he had been,' she said vindictively.

As the police car moved off a few minutes later Pollard turned round. As he expected, its departure was being observed from behind net curtains.

'Let's give her a tootle on the horn,' he remarked to Toye. 'Much though I'd like to kick that blighter Sandford's bottom for trying to hold out on us last night, I've got some fellow feeling for him at this moment. Let's head for the bank before it packs it in for the weekend.'

The bank manager's severely functional room was a relief after Mrs Trevor-Montley's stuffy congested flat. The manager, a Mr Calthrop, was a donnish type given to economy of speech. He listened to Pollard's statement of his business, read Robert Hoyle's authorisation of the removal of the Ambercombe plate box, and summoned a Mr Parry over his intercom.

'This is our Mr Parry,' he informed Pollard, when a middle-aged man appeared. 'He has special responsibility for client's property deposited with us for safe custody. Detective-Superintendent Pollard and Detective-Inspector Toye, Mr Parry. They have an authorisation from Mr Hoyle to remove the plate box belonging to Ambercombe church. Would you get it up for us?'

Mr Parry placed Pollard and Toye in the context of the Ambercombe murder, glanced at them with fascinated speculation, and withdrew with a decorous murmur of 'Certainly, Mr Calthrop.'

'As far as I can remember the plate is withdrawn regularly for the chief church festivals,' the latter said. 'In my early days here Mr Viney himself used to collect it. You'll have heard all about him, of course. A most remarkable old chap.'

'Was the late Miss Ethel Ridd one of your clients?' Pollard asked.

'No, she wasn't. Nor did she come in on Mr Viney's business, it seems. The staff were talking about it after she was murdered, poor woman. After he couldn't get a renewal of his driving licence, someone from Ambercombe used to bring in his cheques to be cashed, with a covering note. Isn't that right, Mr Parry?'

'Yes, Mr Calthrop,' the cashier replied, depositing a battered leather-covered box on a side table. 'A youngish gentleman used to come: the same one who withdrew this plate box for Mr Viney on one occasion.'

Pollard experienced the mental equivalent of a sudden electric shock.

'Do you by any chance keep those notes authorising the bearer to withdraw things from your strong room?' he asked.

'Certainly we do.' A look of disquiet came into Mr Calthrop's face as he stared at Pollard. 'And also, of course, the receipts signed by the person making the withdrawal.'

'May I see the ones relating to this box, then?'

Mr Parry vanished again in response to a nod.

'Does this mean that you suspect that somebody took this box out on a forged authorisation?' Mr Calthrop demanded, by now looking appalled.

'I think it's possible,' Pollard said cautiously.

'But what on earth for? Mr Viney said more than once that the plate was of no great value.'

'The official plate isn't – or so I've been informed. But you may remember that at the Consistory Court of the petition for a faculty to sell it, Miss Ridd insisted that there was another chalice, of which there's no record and no trace. She stated that it had "jewels stuck in it".'

While Mr Calthrop was momentarily speechless, Mr Parry returned with a folder which he placed before Pollard.

'I think you'll find everything in order, sir.'

In a tense silence Pollard and Toye worked back through the recent notes authorising the removal of the plate box, each with a signed receipt attached. The first one in Barnabas Viney's elderly but perfectly legible handwriting was dated 30 May 1974, and had been presented by Margaret Gillard. She had also withdrawn the box before Easter in the same year, and on 13 December 1973. The next receipt, dated 8 August 1973, however, was signed by W. R. Sandford, in whose name the accompanying letter of authorisation was made out. Pollard extracted it, and passed it over to Mr Calthrop.

'What do you make of this?' he asked.

The bank manager studied it at length with a magnifying glass. Finally he looked up with a grim expression.

'Almost certainly a forgery, but I couldn't swear to it, of course. I'm not a handwriting expert.'

'Neither am I,' Pollard replied. 'We must get one on to it at once.'

As he expected, Mr Calthrop demurred at handing over papers belonging to the bank without reference to higher authority, but finally agreed to do so.

'I'll give you a receipt,' Pollard said. 'By the way, there's no question of a valuable chalice having been stolen from the plate box in August 1973. Assuming that Miss Ridd was speaking the truth in the Consistory Court, Mr Viney used it on the morning of June the eleventh, 1974, just before he died.'

'God only knows what the bank's liability could turn out to be, all the same,' Mr Calthrop said gloomily. 'I suppose W. R. Sandford wanted a good look at it to see if it was worth pinching at a convenient moment. Didn't they find old Viney dead on the floor of his church after a service?'

'They did,' Pollard replied, as he got up to go. 'But anything connected with this alleged unrecorded chalice is pure guesswork at the moment. Apart from that one remark of Ethel Ridd's there's no definite evidence that it ever existed. We'll let you know what the handwriting johnny says about this authorisation, and if he's prepared to give an opinion in court that it's a forgery, we'll be confronting Sandford with it, of course. Meanwhile, I know we can rely on your discretion.'

As the Hillman nosed its way through the traffic Toye remarked glumly that they semed to be heading for square one.

'Sandford couldn't have killed Ridd. But it's beginning to look as though he lifted the chalice, and if he did, bang goes the idea that the thief was the murderer.'

'I couldn't have put it more devastatingly clearly myself, old man,' Pollard answered. 'Still, if we're on the wrong track, the only thing to do is to get off it, p.d.q. I suppose there's a chance that we may get the chalice back.'

He spoke bracingly, but was feeling increasingly frustrated by his lack of progress. There was absolutely no dodging the fact that the elimination of Bill Sandford had left them without a single likely suspect, despite the limited field. It simply must be someone knowing the ground and her routine, he thought, as Toye turned into the car park at the police station.

The staff of Westbridge's small forensic department reacted enthusiastically to the prospect of doing another job for Detective-Superintendent Tom Pollard of the Yard. Toye unlocked the plate box with the key lent by Robert Hoyle, and raised its hinged lid.

'Bit of a makeshift job,' Detective-Sergeant Ringer commented.

It was clear that the box had not been made for the express purpose of holding Ambercombe's Georgian plate. There were no slots to keep the various pieces in place, and these, rather sketchily wrapped in chamois leather, were loose inside and did not quite fill it. The padded velvet lining had once been white, but was now yellowed with age.

'You want us to see if there's any sign of another item having been fitted in with this little lot, sir?' Sergeant Ringer summed up.

'That's the idea,' Pollard replied. 'It would have been there for some years, and until seventeeen months ago. Don't bother about dabs. Both the box and the plate have been handled by any number of people. We'll look in again later.'

Inspector Frost was located without much delay, but putting him into the picture was time-consuming, and it transpired that the nearest accredited handwriting expert was at Marchester. A telephone call produced the information that

100

he was at a conference in London, and would not be available until mid-morning on the following day. All that could be done was to despatch the documents from the bank by car, accompanied by an urgent request for the expert's attention at the earliest possible moment.

'Let's get back to the lab,' Pollard said as they extricated themselves from Inspector Frost's room. 'Not that I should think there's a hope in hell that they've managed to get anything from that bloody box,' he added, with an uncharacteristic edge to his voice.

Followed by Toye he went in quietly, and stood by the door. There was an atmosphere of absorbed concentration. Powerful lights were focused on the plate box, now empty and upended, and Sergeant Ringer was engaged in close-up photography of its interior. No one spoke. Pollard was aware of a quickened heart beat. Then the shutter of the camera clicked and the Sergeant straightened up.

'You're bang on, sir,' he said. 'Come and take a look for yourself. The items were fitted in quite differently, long enough for the sharp edges to make these grooves in the velvet. That gave enough room for the missing object to lie diagonally in this top left-hand corner. See, sir?'

Pollard and Toye, poring over the plate box, saw. The large, rather clumsy Georgian chalice, the two matching cruets and the pair of candlesticks had also been wedged in diagonally.

'From these marks up here in the corner, what sort of a missing object would you say it was, Sergeant?' Pollard asked, trying to suppress his excitement.

'I'd say it was another of these tall cups, sir. Chalices, aren't they? Much smaller, though. Quite a little 'un ... give us that rule, Jim ... Say five inches tall, sir. There's where the edge of the cup cut in, and there's the circular mark of the foot.'

Catching sight of the expression on Pollard's face, Sergeant Ringer grinned broadly.

'Have we told you what you wanted to hear, sir? Mind you, we'll have to measure up accurately for our official report.'

'Man,' Pollard assured him, 'you've given us the best bit

101

of news we've had since we were sent down here.'

Back in their room Pollard flung himself down on a chair. He sat with hands clasped behind his head and long legs stretched out under the table for nearly a minute. Finally he looked across at Toye with the air of having arrived at a decision.

'I'll buy it, provisionally,' he said.

Toye expressed cautious agreement.

'So what?' Pollard went on. 'If that service on June the eleventh, 1974 was at 11.00 a.m., and there was only a congregation of one, it must have been over by 11.30. Ethel Ridd goes back to the vicarage to get the vegetarian lunch, leaving Viney to put things away and say his prayers. She bursts into the Barton saying she's found him lying on the church floor just as Matthew Gillard comes in for the farm dinner at 12.30. Say at 12.25, the discovery having been made at 12.20, by which time the chalice has vanished. What happened during those fifty minutes?'

'Either the old gentleman managed to hide away the chalice so that it's never been found, or someone came in and made off with it,' Toye replied unhesitatingly.

'Agreed. In theory he could have popped out and buried it in the churchyard, but that simply doesn't tie up with all the elaborate arrangements for keeping it safely in the bank. And you've seen the church. It's minute, and built of large solid blocks of stone, with a stone floor. No handy loose bricks to pull out. The chalice wasn't in the cupboard – we've Mrs Gillard's evidence on that, and I vetted the pulpit and the font. So it looks as though, as you say, someone came in and lifted the thing.'

'Before or after Mr Viney collapsed and died?' Toye queried.

'It wouldn't take much to give an old chap of eighty-eight a fatal heart attack,' Pollard said thoughtfully. 'Just a show of force, for instance. On the other hand, someone may have come in, found him on the floor with the chalice beside him, and just appropriated it and walked out again.'

'Somebody being Sandford?'

'Apart from Ethel Ridd's hiker, Sandford's the only candidate at the moment, isn't he? We're taking it that he'd illegally checked up on the chalice, and no doubt knew about the services Viney had on Saints' days.'

Toye looked up from his diary.

'June the eleventh 1974 was a Monday. Sandford works at the College here on Mondays this year. Do these places change their timetables much?'

'Easy to find out. But I'm not making a move until we hear from the handwriting bloke. While we're marking time let's look into the exact circumstances of Viney's death. There may have been an inquest. He doesn't sound like the sort of chap who'd have much use for doctors.'

An enquiry resulted in the information that an inquest had been held on Barnabas James Viney on Friday 15 June 1974, and a report of its proceedings was soon forthcoming. There had been a verdict of death from natural causes, the immediate cause being a severe cerebral haemorrhage. Evidence on the finding of the body was given incoherently by Ethel Ridd, and clearly and sensibly by Matthew Henry and Emily Margaret Gillard. Deceased had fallen face downwards at the back of the church, by the cupboard in the recess under the belfry. His head and shoulders were lying in the aisle between the first pair of benches, suggesting that he was on the point of walking up the aisle when he fell. He had removed his stole and surplice, put them away in the cupboard with the various articles used in the service, and locked the cupboard. The key had been found on the floor beside him. Dr William Bruce Jarvis, of Ford House, Pyrford, who had arrived at the church a few minutes ahead of the ambulance, stated that he had attended the deceased in February 1970, when he was suffering from pneumonia, but had not seen him professionally since. Mr Viney had made a remarkable recovery, but he (Dr Jarvis) had warned him that his blood pressure was above normal. Mr Viney, however, had refused to have periodical checks made. In Dr Jarvis's opinion death had been virtually instantaneous, resulting from a severe cerebral haemorrhage affecting the right side of the body and producing marked flaccidity of the facial muscles. This opinion had subsequently been confirmed by a post-mortem held at Westbridge General Hospital, at which no other cause of death had been found.

103

'Straightforward, from the look of it,' Toye commented.

Pollard made a vague assenting noise, wondering why he felt inexplicably dissatisfied.

'I suppose a stroke as well as a heart attack can be sparked off by a shock?' he queried. 'Suppose somebody came in at the door and told the old chap to hand over – or else? Let's look up this Dr Jarvis tomorrow morning. It's just possible we might get something, I suppose. Anyway, isn't he on Frost's List C? We could have to go back to it, and start all over again.'

Toye, dedicated to methodical procedure, welcomed the suggestion.

Dr Jarvis's surgery at Pyrford occupied an annexe to his house. Through the co-operation of Mrs Jarvis, Pollard and Toye by-passed the queue of waiting patients and arrived in the consulting room through an inner door. The doctor, grizzled and weatherbeaten, got up from his desk and greeted them with undisguised interest.

'I've seen you around,' he said, 'and thought you'd be along sooner or later. This is where my profession goes all correct and sticky in the whodunits, isn't it? Is it poor old Ridd you're after, or my failure to find a witness to my whereabouts the afternoon she was bumped off?'

'Actually, it's the late Barnabas Viney,' Pollard told him.

'*Barnabas Viney?*' Dr Jarvis ejaculated. 'Why, all that business seems a hundred years ago after what's been happening round here lately. I didn't do the P-M, you know. That was Craig, one of the Westbridge police surgeons.'

'I know: I've read the report of the inquest. Just one question, Doctor. Could the stroke he died of have been brought on by a sudden shock? Like somebody turning up and threatening him, for instance?'

'But what the hell would anybody have wanted to threaten the poor old blighter about?' Dr Jarvis demanded incredulously. 'He looked as though he hadn't a brass farthing in his pocket and needed a good square meal. Well, yes, to answer your question, a sudden violent emotional reaction could have triggered off a stroke in a chap of his age, especially one with fairly high blood pressure. You'll have read my

104

reference to his blood pressure in the inquest report. But I can only say that there was absolutely nothing in the way he was lying or in his expression to suggest that he'd been terrified by anything or anybody. Naturally I should have drawn attention to it if there had been.'

'Fair enough. Thanks for being so helpful,' Pollard replied soothingly. 'Now, just for good measure, can you add to your original statement on what you did on the afternoon of the nineteenth?'

'As it happens, I can. I meant to get on to Frost, but I've been snowed under. Wednesday's my day off, and I spent most of it down at Coracle Bay Bird Sanctuary. Jim Doulton, the Warden, rang me about something else last night, and asked if I'd spotted anything interesting. He'd been away all day but noticed my car in a lay-by when he came back about four. I stayed late to watch the Canada geese coming down the valley to the shore marshes, and got home here about six.'

'Thanks for clearing up that loose end, too,' Pollard said.

Back in the car Toye made a neat entry by Dr Jarvis's name on List C. Pollard looked at his watch. It was still barely ten o'clock: much too early to try to contact the handwriting expert. He felt his edginess of the previous evening returning, aggravated by indecision. After all, he had been sent down to solve the Ridd murder, but seemed to be continually diverted on to the problem of the missing chalice's existence and present whereabouts. Yet even now, when Sandford, the likely thief, was unquestionably in the clear over the murder, his own hunch that the two problems were somehow linked was stronger than ever.

Toye had regrouped the names on List C geographically, and at his suggestion they took a steep left turn at the bottom of Pyrford's main street.

'What's a water vole?' he asked, as he changed down.

'A water vole? What on earth – ? Oh, yes. The Redshaw woman's drivelling poems,' Pollard replied. 'It's a sort of water rat with a long tail ... This place stinks of money, doesn't it? Just as Hoyle said.'

They had swung right into an immaculate drive leading to a terrace in front of an eighteenth-century stone house in mint condition. As they got out of the car Toye looked back at a palatial garage reached by a branch from the main drive.

'Room for six cars in there. Wish I could have a look inside,' he said, almost wistfully.

'Keep your mind on the job,' Pollard admonished him in tones of mock reproof. 'Stand by to chat up the lady about water voles.'

He found the white and gold drawing room into which they were ushered self-consciously elegant. The same could be said of Miranda Redshaw, who rose to greet them in a long flowing garment of cream-coloured woollen material. As Pollard introduced himself and the purpose of his visit a pained expression replaced the cultivated serenity of her face.

'I know nothing of this hideous affair, nothing,' she assured him, gazing at him with soulful blue eyes. 'I find even the mention of it distasteful. I try to make this house a place of peace and beauty.'

'I expect Miss Ridd found being murdered distasteful,' he was goaded into retorting, and instantly regretted the lapse. Detective-Superintendent Crow, one of his earliest mentors at the Yard, had warned him about antagonising witnesses, remarking that unless you wanted them to clam up, it paid to keep your cool, however bloody-minded they were. He hastily pulled himself together. It was fantastic to think of this woman bashing Ethel Ridd on the head with a brick, so he concentrated on the time of her husband's return home.

Confirmation of Martha Rook's statement was forthcoming at once. The sound of the car coming up the drive had coincided with the church clock striking five.

'Did he go out again that evening?' Pollard asked Miranda Redshaw.

She shook her head and smiled, subtly suggesting a lack of comprehension on his part.

'We are both creative writers, you see, and the visit to Marchester had been such an interruption. Apart from our supper, we spent the evening at our desks.'

The sound of a door opening and a masculine tread in the hall suggested that the household's creative writing had

106

suffered another interruption. A red-faced man with a tooth-brush moustache and wearing expensive looking tweeds walked into the room.

'What goes on?' he demanded. 'By Jove, the great man from the Yard! How dare you hog him, Miranda? This is the chance of a lifetime for a crime hack like me. Introduce us, darling.'

She complied, murmuring *sotto voce* to Pollard that her husband was a great big boy. He treasured up the remark for Jane, wondering if this was Miranda Redshaw's technique for accepting her husband and his lurid books. Not to mention the income from them, he thought . . .

After some further badinage from Hugh Redshaw, the three men moved at his suggestion to his study, which struck Pollard as a perfect stage set for a play about a successful author. It was all there: vast desk littered with typescript, typewriter, dictaphone, well-filled bookshelves, conspicuously displayed copies of the author's works.

Hugh Redshaw sank into a leather-covered arm chair facing his visitors, and assumed the expression of an intelligent man determined not to miss the slightest detail of the impending interview.

'Now I shall really know how one is grilled,' he told them avidly.

Pollard once again took a firm grip on his temper. He consulted his watch.

'Nothing that's likely to come in for your books, I'm afraid, Mr Redshaw,' he said pleasantly. 'Just a quick run-through of the statement you made to the local police about your movements on the nineteenth. Routine, you know. The sort of time-consuming job you writers can telescope . . . I see that your departure from the bar of the Cathedral Hotel at about 1.50 p.m. is well documented.'

Hugh Redshaw guffawed, and gave Pollard a man-to-man look.

'Naughty of me, I'm afraid, but these provincial coppers, y' know. He took it all down: name, address and telephone number of the friend I'd been talking to. But I did pick up one tip: he didn't suck a pencil. The chap actually had a biro. One has to try to keep up to date.'

'The price of being with-it is eternal vigilance,' Pollard agreed. 'You then went on to the public library, to check some references, but are not sure when you left?'

'Not absolutely. One rather loses count of time in these places. Gets sidetracked. But it was twenty-five to four when I left the station car park.'

'What is your car, Mr Redshaw?'

Hugh Redshaw subtly conveyed that he was amused by the question.

'Let me think ... yes, I took the Mercedes in. Not the Jag.'

'And you took almost an hour and a half to get back here from Marchester in a Mercedes?'

Hugh Redshaw slapped his knee triumphantly.

'Thank God you've left me my illusions. The Yard is characteristically bang on. I came the long way round to pick up a couple of ducks at Breakacres Farm, where we get our poultry. Free range, y' see. The ducks are pure ambrosia. It's about five miles to the north of here. The bobby completely missed out on the time factor.'

'And you arived here at five o'clock?'

'On the dot. The church clock was striking as I turned up from the village green.'

'Did you go out again that night?'

'Not on your life. It had been quite a day. I went to ground in here,' Hugh Redshaw added, with a jerk of his head in the direction of an obvious drinks cabinet, and a broad wink.

Shortly afterwards, as the Hillman negotiated the abrupt descent to the village, Pollard designated Hugh Redshaw a prize bastard.

'That damn awful phoney female, too,' he said. 'Look here, I'm going to have a bash at Marchester. This messing about is getting me down. Pull up by that telephone kiosk.'

The kiosk had been recently redecorated and its interior, flooded with morning sunlight, was still pristine, and reminded Pollard of a hospital. He got through to Marchester police station without difficulty, and heard almost with incredulity that Mr Bramber had already come in, and could take a call. He held the line as requested, and in less than a minute a dry elderly voice came over the line.

'Yes, an interesting little job you've sent over,' it said, after an exchange of formalities. 'An obvious forgery, of course. Not a doubt in the world. Overall, and at first glance it's quite effective, but there's a curious disregard of minor details. It's more like an artist's impression of the original than an attempt at a meticulous reproduction, if you follow me . . .'

As he rang off, it flashed through Pollard's mind, not for the first time in his career, what a catalyst a few sentences could be.

'Full steam ahead,' he told Toye as he rejoined him in the car. 'At any rate we ought to get this chalice business off our hands by tonight.'

'The 1974 timetable?' David Longstaffe, head of the history department at the Westbridge College of Education queried. 'Yes, we can soon unearth it for you.'

There was a short interval during which his secretary searched and found a printed form, and placed it before him.

'This ran from October '73 to the end of the academic year,' David Longstaffe said, as the door closed behind her. 'Any particular day or time?'

'This is a confidential enquiry,' Pollard told him. 'We want to know if Mr Sandford worked here on Mondays during the summer of '74.'

David Longstaffe, a grey balding man with rimless spectacles looked surprised, but refrained from comment.

'Yes, he did,' he replied, on referring to the timetable, 'have you one special Monday in mind? Of course, at this distance of time I can't swear that he wasn't off sick or had leave of absence for some reason.'

'We're interested in the morning of Monday, June the eleventh.'

A subtle change of expression came over David Longstaffe's face.

'Hold on a minute,' he said, and stooped to hunt in a drawer. He extracted a large diary, and began turning its pages.

'Ah, I thought so,' he said. 'Sandford wasn't around on June the eleventh. He left with a party of students on June the eighth for a fortnight in Greece.'

The ensuing silence was long enough to make him glance up at the two impassive faces confronting him across his desk.

'Thanks, Mr Longstaffe,' Pollard said. 'That's the information we wanted. We'd like a word with Mr Sandford. Is he free at the moment?'

'He's due out of a lecture in five minutes. See him in here, if you like. I'm just off to a committee.'

'That's very kind: thanks again.'

David Longstaffe snatched up a folder and prepared to depart. At the door he paused briefly, but finally went out without any further remark.

Pollard and Toye sat on in silence for some moments.

'What are the odds that Sandford knew where the chalice must have been hidden, and picked it up when he got back?' Toye asked.

'There was that hiker,' Pollard said. 'Suppose he was a chap dead set on seeing the church, came back when he thought the service would be over, and found Viney and the chalice on the floor?'

The door opened and Bill Sandford stopped dead on the threshold.

'Where's Longstaffe? I was told he wanted to see me.'

'He's lent us this room for a talk,' Pollard replied. 'Come in, Mr Sandford, and sit down.'

Bill Sandford strolled across and subsided nonchalantly into the desk chair.

'Well, what is it now?' he demanded. 'I imagine you've checked my alibi for Ridd's murder and found it holds water.'

'It does,' Pollard told him. 'We've had an interesting visit to the West Regional Bank, though, and forensic tests have been made on the Ambercombe plate box. Why did you forge an authorisation to withdraw it from the bank on August the eighth, 1973?'

After a fleeting reaction of astonishment. Bill Sandford gave Pollard a look of grudging admiration.

'Nifty work on your part,' he said. 'How did you get on to it? Oh, I forgot: you're here to ask questions, not answer them, aren't you? I wanted to have a look inside. I'm an enquiring sort of bloke, you know.'

'You knew that Mr Viney used an unrecorded chalice on occasions?'

Bill Sandford grimaced and shrugged.

'I'd better come clean, I suppose. I'd seen the thing. The east window of the church is plain glass, and I happened to cut through the vicarage garden and the churchyard one morning just when he was – elevating, I believe the expression is – the chalice at one of his weekday services. I know a bit about church plate, and saw at once that it wasn't the Victorian or Georgian one. And when the old boy dried up when I asked him about it, well, I got curious. But you've nothing on me. I took the bloody box back with its contents intact, didn't I? And –'

'You were abroad on the morning when Mr Viney died, and the chalice Miss Ridd spoke of had been in use,' Pollard cut in quickly, once again depriving Bill Sandford of playing the ace of trumps. He changed his tactics abruptly. 'What do you think has happened to it, Mr Sandford?'

He got a sulky but astonished glare.

'Pretty obvious, isn't it? Ridd nicked it and stowed it away as a holy relic. She was nuts on Viney. I don't mind admitting that I've managed to get inside the vicarage and her cottage once or twice, and had a look round, but she'd got a half-wit's cunning. Why the hell don't you take her place to pieces instead of hounding me?'

Taken aback by a possibility which had never occurred to him, Pollard rallied quickly.

'You're in a very dicey position, Mr Sandford,' he observed.

'Don't I know it? That's why I thought I'd better keep my mouth shut and try to find the thing on my own. Now you know what's happened, for God's sake do something about it. It may be deteriorating in some filthy damp hole. It's a genuine medieval chalice, and I swear the stones in it are rubies, not glass. Here's my key. Search my place, if you like.'

111

He flung down a latch key and banged out of the room. Pollard made no attempt to stop him.

'How much of that do you swallow?' Toye asked.

'Not the Ridd bit necessarily, although it's a possibility, I suppose. But I don't think he's got the chalice, you know. Let's go to Ambercombe, old man,' he added, as Toye looked interrogative. 'We'll pick up Ridd's key and a few tools at the station. We've done some pretty effective search jobs before, haven't we? And if we end up with nothing by tonight, we'll drop the blasted chalice and start all over again.'

Toye tactfully forbore to ask what the new starting point would be. After a brief call at the police station they set out for Ambercombe once more.

Pollard leant back in the car, feeling that his brain was impossibly congested with unco-ordinated data. He shut his eyes, hoping that a sifting process might sort things out. To his surprise he found himself at once trying to visualise in detail the back of the church, but without success. On impulse, when they drew up at the gate, he told Toye that they'd better have a look round inside first before going on to the cottage.

Two minutes later he was standing at the top of the tiny aisle looking towards the west wall. Yes, there was the locked cupboard in the recess under the belfry, and there was a table with magazines or something on it on the right. The font was in the angle between the west and south walls. Very little spare space. He stared at the cupboard. Suddenly a stab of excitement went through him.

'Here,' he said abruptly. 'Just take up the position of Viney's body, will you? By the cupboard, and your head and shoulders in the aisle.'

Toye complied.

'No. That won't work. Mrs Gillard couldn't have opened the cupboard door more than an inch or two. It opens from right to left. Try the other side, with your feet by the font ... Toye, what was he doing coming away from the font? He'd already put everything away in the cupboard and locked it.'

Pollard lifted off the oak font cover and put it on the floor, peered into the dusty uncommunicative stone bowl, innocent of everything but dust, a dried leaf or two and a scurrying spider. He stooped and picked up the dark oak cover again. It was dome-shaped, with carved external ribs running up to a small turret-like erection at the top. This was surmounted by a cross.

'Outside,' Pollard said briefly.

In the churchyard they inverted the cover. It was very dusty, and spiders' webs had collected under the top. Toye produced a tissue and removed them. A circular piece of wood had been carefully inserted about four inches below the opening of the turret.

'We want a knife with a thin blade,' Pollard said. 'Remember that the Archdeacon said old Viney went in for carpentry?'

Toye, skilful with his hands, removed the piece of wood without difficulty.

'All yours, sir,' he said a little breathlessly.

Pollard cautiously withdrew something wrapped in tissue paper.

It was a small chalice of silver gilt with a shallow bowl. A tiny crucifix was beautifully engraved on the circular foot. The metal was a little dulled by months of neglect, but the rubies, set in the form of a cross on one side of the bowl, caught the sunlight and flashed it back. A piece of writing paper had fallen to the ground.

'Found in Ambercombe vicarage garden in Holy Week 1960,' it said laconically, in the handwriting of Barnabas Viney ...

After a short interval Toye characteristically raised the question of practical action.

'Well,' he said, 'I suppose we start hunting for that hiker for want of a better lead. All the same, I can't for the life of me see how it ties up with this chalice. If he was after it why did he come back all set to murder Ridd? It didn't even look as though he was trying to get her to talk.'

'This is it,' Pollard said, carefully wrapping the chalice in a clean handkerchief.

Suddenly he gave an incoherent exclamation and stared at Toye.

'My God, I've only just seen it! We've been on the wrong tack the whole time. She was done for blowing the gaff about the *hiker*, not the chalice.'

Chapter 9

'So you propose making a television appearance, Pollard?'

The Assistant Commissioner's ironic inflexion was a well-known sign of satisfaction with progress made.

'I feel it's probably the most effective way of getting a line on Ethel Ridd's hiker, sir,' Pollard replied tactfully. 'The chalice having turned up will get local people interested, and when they're asked if they noticed a hiker around on June the eleventh 1974, they'll be readier to make the effort to think back. We're collecting facts to bring the day to their minds. For instance, there was a bad car smash on the West-bridge side of Pyrford at about six that morning, and the road was blocked for a couple of hours and normal traffic held up. People remember having their plans and routine disorganised.'

The AC grunted and relapsed into silence.

'You seriously think you've uncovered a second murder?' he asked, after a lengthy pause.

'I think the odds are that this hiker chap was murdered on or soon after June the eleventh, 1974, and vanished without trace until inconveniently resurrected by Ethel Ridd in the Consistory Court on November the nineteenth this year. The theory I'm working on at the moment is that his killer was present, and decided that her mouth had to be shut before an interested press started probing. You see, sir, she'd mentioned him almost in the same breath with a valu-able missing chalice: an absolute gift to newsmen on the look-out for a story.'

'Since the chalice has turned out to be a red herring in the investigation of Ethel Ridd's murder, presumably the same applies in relation to the hiker's – if this took place,' the AC said thoughtfully. 'You argue – convincingly, in my opinion – that her killer had the sort of detailed knowledge of her movements that only a local resident could possess. You've interviewed quite a number of these. Have you formed the slightest suspicion of anyone being involved in something that would lend itself to blackmail, for instance?'

'There's a chap called Aldridge, sir, who runs the village shops, and who lied about his movements in the early afternoon of November the nineteenth, but on grounds of timing it doesn't seem possible for him to have murdered Ethel Ridd. Of course we don't know whether he, or anyone else with an alibi for that matter, also has one for the morning of June the eleventh, 1974, and it's not going to be easy to find out at this distance of time. And I suppose one can't entirely rule out the possibility of two murderers acting in collusion. Anyway, as I said just now, I feel the immediate step is to try and find out if and where and when anybody saw a hiker around at that time.'

The AC commented incisively on the time and manpower that the new stage of the enquiry would take up.

'And don't overlook the spate of irrelevant and lunatic letters and telephone calls that your TV act will produce,' he added grimly. 'Am I to understand that this Archdeacon Lacy has agreed to appear with you?'

'Not *with* me, sir. It's really his show. The story of the chalice and so on. He'll have it on view, and touch indirectly on Ambercombe's repair problems. Not a formal appeal, of course, but he thinks some unsolicited contributions might come in.'

'I always maintain that the children of this world have nothing on the children of light, given a promising opening. Then you follow on, I take it?'

'That's the idea, sir. We thought he could bring me on as the chap who actually found the chalice. I'd then touch on old Mr Viney's death being the result of heaving the font cover about, and say we'd like to talk to the hiker who looked in during the service. Would he come forward, or anyone who remembers seeing him around that morning.'

The AC pressed a switch on his desk and summoned his secretary, indicating that the interview was at an end.

'Well, Pollard, you'd better go ahead. I only hope something will come out of it over and above increased publicity for yourself.'

116

Pollard hastily extricated himself with thanks as the secretary materialised.

'And keep me posted,' the AC called after him as he reached the door.

'Certainly, sir,' he replied, suppressing a grin as he went out to join Toye, who was engaged in studying the record of persons reported missing in the early summer of 1974.

There proved to be a daunting number of these of possible hiking age, and at the moment all that could be done was to compile a list. Pollard looked at it gloomily.

'How about the blokes whose disappearances weren't reported?' he asked. 'Here, let's push off home for a few hours. See you on the train.'

Jane Pollard's reaction to her husband's forthcoming television venture took him aback.

'What tie will you wear?' she demanded.

'*Tie?*'

'Of course. The chaps who read the news have made the whole country tie-conscious. Kenneth Kendall and Richard Baker and all that crowd. Why, people round here are keeping records of individual totals, and I know several families who've gone over to colour because they felt they were missing half the fun. And by the way, you could do with a haircut.'

'Fortunately,' he told her, 'you won't see me.'

'What do you mean?'

'I'll only be on the Regional News, you know.'

'Tom! What an absolute swindle! Couldn't I write to the BBC or whatever and ask if I might take the twins along and have a run-through of the film?'

'If you do, I'll leave you ... Oh, God, they've woken up!' he added, as thumps were audible overhead.

'It must have been quite a moment when you realised that you'd found the chalice Miss Ridd had spoken about in the Consistory Court,' the television interviewer suggested helpfully.

'It certainly was,' Pollard agreed, feeling unexpectedly at ease under the powerful lighting of the studio. 'In fact, I could hardly take it in for a second or two. Unfortunately, though, I'm down here on a much less pleasant job than discovering missing treasure. My assignment is to track down the killer of the late Miss Ethel Ridd, who was brutally murdered on November the nineteenth in Ambercombe vicarage, and I've come along this evening to ask for help from you people' – turning his head to address his invisible audience – 'who are viewing this programme. We want to talk to the hiker who came into Ambercombe church at about a quarter past eleven on the morning of Tuesday, June the eleventh, 1974. If he was a local man, will he, please, contact us, either by ringing Westbridge 4321 Extension 4, or through any police station. A service was going on, and he went out again almost at once. He could have been a visitor on holiday, of course, and in this case he probably won't be viewing at this moment, and this is where some of you may be able to help us contact him. Will you try to put your minds back to June the eleventh last year? It may sound a tall order, but for residents in the Pyrford and Ambercombe area it was a memorable day. It started off with the pile-up on the Westbridge road, which was blocked with wreckage for nearly two hours. Later in the morning the Reverend Barnabas Viney, vicar of Ambercombe, collapsed and died in his church. These events may help you to remember what you were doing, and if you noticed a hiker around, or a strange car parked anywhere. Did you travel on the Westbridge bus and happen to notice a hiker among your fellow passengers?

'If you can remember anything that may be helpful to us, please ring me, Detective-Superintendent Tom Pollard, at Westbridge police station. I'll just give you the number again ...'

This interview, recorded at the television studios on Tuesday morning, was screened during the Regional News programme at 6 p.m. the same evening, following Archdeacon Lacy's lively account of the history, and discovery by Pollard, of the Tadenham chalice. By half past ten some twenty calls had been made to the Westbridge police, not one of which offered a viable lead. Those which were not patent hoaxes or crackpots were too vague to follow up, and Pollard decided to call it a day. It was not until he and

118

Toye were finishing their breakfast on the following morning that a call came through from the police station, telling him that a woman had rung from North Pyrford to say that she had sold a packet of cigarettes to a hiker on the morning of 11 June in the previous year.

'Funny she's so sure of the exact date after all this time,' Pollard remarked, gulping down the last of his coffee. 'I said we'd go round to the station right away.'

In the Hillman they consulted the inch-to-the-mile ordnance survey map of the district. North Pyrford turned out to be a small hamlet in a valley running down to the Westbridge road from the Whitehallow Hills, about four miles north of Pyrford.

'Can't be much of a shop in a place that size,' Toye commented, 'so a stranger turning up would've been noticed.'

'I'm not sure about that,' Pollard replied, poring over the map. 'Look, the minor road to North Pyrford becomes a sort of farm track higher up the valley, and leads to prehistoric monuments. Hut circles, and a standing stone called The Hollow Man. What price T. S. Eliot, but I expect it's a corruption of Hallow. Seriously, though, quite a lot of people would come up to see these things, and buy crisps and sweets and fags to keep themselves going. Hence the unlikely shop, I expect.'

Toye agreed cautiously that it could be.

At the police station they were told that the woman who had rung in, a Mrs Hayball, was short of breath and a bit hard of hearing into the bargain.

'Asthma, from the sound of it,' the sergeant reported, 'and not all that easy to make out what she was saying. Still, she was quite definite about the date when she sold a hiker chap a packet of fags, sir. She's not on the phone herself, but there's a call box next to the shop.'

'We'll go over,' Pollard decided after deliberating briefly. 'Unless anything more promising has come in?'

'Nothing so far this morning, sir. Only a kid trying it on. I blasted the little perisher good and proper.'

'Nice work,' Pollard approved. 'We'll be off, then, Sergeant. Try ringing the call box if we're wanted.'

*

It was a wretched morning of drizzling rain. As Pollard sat watching the windscreen wipers coping with mud splashes from passing cars, he mentally reviewed the inhabitants of Pyrford and Ambercombe already known to him. There would be talk following his broadcast. Suppose an unguarded remark by somebody were to lead to a third murder, once again with the aim of shutting a dangerous mouth for good? Suddenly the burden of his responsibility became almost intolerable. They were running into Pyrford now, and as they passed the rectory and Dr Jarvis's surgery he wondered why on earth he had elected to go into the police.

Just beyond the entrance to the village green Toye halted at the tail of a gaggle held up by the clumsy manoeuvring of the school bus. After several boss shots it succeeded in turning by backing into a gateway beyond the Pyrford Garage on their right, and finally lumbered into an adjacent lay-by, nose to Westbridge in readiness for the afternoon run. Toye swept ahead by a skilful outflanking movement, uttering caustic comment. The road ran northwards along the foot of the Whitehallow Hills, the tops of which were shrouded in mist. On their left were level fields, lifeless except for an occasional herd of Friesians sheltering from the persistent light rain in the lee of a hedge, patient, with drooping heads.

'About another half-mile,' Toye said presently, breaking a long silence.

Pollard surfaced, and almost at once a road sign came into view. They slowed for a sharp right turn, and passed a substantial farmhouse and its outbuildings before beginning to gain height. After a quarter of a mile the gradient flattened out slightly, and a cluster of cottages appeared, with a few modern bungalows on its outskirts. In the general greyness a post office telephone kiosk's cheerful red shone out like a beacon, and Toye parked on an unoccupied patch of rough grass beside it.

Over the front door of a cottage close to the kiosk was a white board, with the barely perceptible legend C. HAYBALL. NEWSAGENT in black lettering. The door stood open. Inside, on the left, another door was labelled SHOP. Pollard turned its handle, set an old-fashioned bell on a strip of metal jangling, and stepped down into a musty dimness redolent of paraffin.

'Anyone at home?' he called.

An electric light bulb suspended from the ceiling at the back of the shop was switched on. Standing in a doorway behind a counter was the fattest woman he had ever seen, her torso suggesting the trunk of a massive oak tree. A cascade of chins descended from her enormous good-humoured red face. She surveyed Pollard with little black eyes peering out between rolls of flesh.

'Mrs Hayball?' he asked, recovering from initial shock and walking forward.

'That's me. Clara Hayball, the North Pyrford heavy-weight, they calls me round 'ere. You'll be the gentleman from Scotland Yard on the telly last night. My, you came over beautiful. I'd've rung sooner, but I was over to me son's . . .'

A fit of wheezing and coughing interrupted her narrative. When it subsided, Pollard hastily thanked her for contacting the police, wondering how long it was going to take to get any coherent information from her at this rate.

'That's better,' she said. 'Proper old nuisance, me asthma, and they don't seem to be able to do nothin' about it. Please to come through: 'tis warmer and more private, like.'

She lifted the counter flap, and Pollard and Toye followed her into a snug living room with a good fire on the hearth. Sinking into a vast armchair she waved her visitors to seats.

'How is it you remember so clearly selling a packet of cigarettes to a hiker on the date I was talking about last night, Mrs Hayball?' Pollard asked.

'I'll tell you for why,' she replied without hesitation. ' 'Twas the morning Mrs Morley up the road got a letter in the post to say she'd won a hundred pound Premium Bond prize. 'E'd hardly gone off when the 'ole village came packin' in to clack about it. Then tea-time it got round about Rev-erend Viney droppin' dead in Ambercombe church. Proper day, it was.'

Further questions established the hiker's arrival at the shop at a few minutes after nine, after the newspapers had been dropped off the van, but just before the mail arrived,

121

which was never more than a minute or two on either side of a quarter past.

'It come when 'e was makin' a phone call,' Mrs Hayball added.

'Who was? The hiker?' Pollard metaphorically sat up.

'That's right. Asked me for small change, 'e did, when 'e paid for the Players.'

'It must have been a local call if he wanted small change,' Toye observed. 'Did he say he'd got friends or relatives round here?'

She shook her head, sending ripples through her double chins.

'Didn't say nothin' about that. Combinin' business and pleasure, 'e said.'

Pollard proceeded to question her with all his skill about the hiker's appearance and characteristics, but without much success. Like most people, she found it almost impossible to give a recognisable description of another human being. The man had been medium tall, looked like somebody who had an outdoor job, not young, but not old either. He'd worn scruffy old fawn jeans, a brown and white check shirt open at the neck, and had a pack on his back. He'd said he was having a walking holiday, sleeping rough at night. How old? Getting along. Say fifty.

'Do you think you'd recognise him if you saw him again?' Pollard asked her.

'I don't know as I should,' she replied doubtfully, 'not unless 'e was togged up the same, that is. A lot comes in summer time, goin' up top to see they old stones. I might reckernise 'is voice though.'

'Why? Was there something special about it, Mrs Hayball?'

' 'E wasn't a foreigner, nor yet a Welshman or from up north, but it didn't sound quite right. More like an American, only not so much.'

Before Pollard could pursue the subject, a strident ringing sound penetrated to the room. Mrs Haybell began to lumber to her feet but was anticipated by Toye.

'Could be a call for us,' he said.

'You cut along and see, love,' Mrs Hayball replied thankfully, sinking back again. 'I can't get around the way I used to. It ain't my son's time for ringing the box.'

He was absent for several minutes before returning and beckoning Pollard into the shop.

'It was Frost, ringing on chance from Ambercombe. That kid Rosemary Gillard has tried to drown herself in the quarry pool, and they found threatening notes on her. He wants us to go over right away.'

Pollard, momentarily immobilised, swore violently. He swung round and went back into the living room.

'We're wanted at Ambercombe, Mrs Hayball,' he said, 'so we'll have to cut along. Later on, you'll be asked to sign a statement of the facts you've given us. You've been very helpful, and we're grateful to you for getting on to us so quickly.'

'That's all right,' she wheezed, leaning forward with avid curiosity in her small eyes. 'Wanted over to Ambercombe in a 'urry, are you?'

'What else did Frost say?' Pollard demanded as soon as he and Toye were clear of the cottage. 'What about the kid?'

'She's been taken to Westbridge Hospital by ambulance. They think she may have hit her head on something when she went in, and concussed herself.'

'What were these threatening notes about?'

'Frost didn't say,' Toye replied, unlocking the car. 'He was short and cagey. I took it he was speaking from the Gillards' place, and people were milling around. But it seemed clear enough that he thought there was a tie-up with our case,' he added, as they moved forward on to the road.

For a time Pollard sat tensely silent.

'If that kid's had it, I'll never forgive myself,' he said suddenly, as Toye slowed down at the road junction. 'There was obviously something seriously wrong: you must have seen it yourself. I ought to have tried to get her to open up.'

They were now heading for Pyrford at a speed which attracted astonished stares from the occupants of overtaken cars.

'It didn't look like a priority lead,' Toye reasoned. He

went on to employ a diversionary tactic. 'It was Sandford who got her out.'

'Sandford? My God, if he's been up to any funny business where she's concerned, I'll have his guts out.'

Toye persevered in his efforts to lower the temperature.

'He could have heard her go in. It's quiet as the grave up by the quarry, and his cottage is the end one.'

Pollard gave a non-committal grunt. His mind had already discarded Bill Sandford, and was back at the possibility of a third murder which had occurred to him so disturbingly earlier that morning, on the way out to North Pyrford. Was a botched attempt at this the real explanation of Rosemary Gillard's landing up in the quarry pool? Or had somebody relied on intimidation through a series of threatening letters to get the girl to kill herself? And was it vital to get her out of the way in case her nerve broke and she let out out that she had seen the hiker?

In his impatience to get at the facts the journey to Ambercombe seemed endless. The drizzle had developed into a relentless downpour, and a streaming road surface and poor visibility compelled Toye to reduce speed. At last they passed through Pyrford, took the Ambercombe hill and swept in at the gate of the Barton. A police car was at the door, and a knot of onlookers huddled under umbrellas had materialised in hopes of witnessing further sensational events.

There was a tense atmosphere in the farm kitchen where Matthew Gillard, whom Pollard identified from Ethel Ridd's funeral, was heatedly confronting Inspector Frost, with the outraged expression of a man involved in an incredible and unprovoked disruption of his normal life.

'... tell me that!' he bellowed, as Pollard and Toye walked in. 'The whole place's lousy with cops, an' all you do is find some bloody old chalice while folk gets their heads bashed in, and my girl's driven to drown herself by threats. What's going on round here? What the hell are you people paid for?'

'Why wasn't Rosemary at school today, Mr Gillard?' Pollard enquired.

The deliberate banality of the question had the desired

effect. Matthew Gillard, struck silent, stared at him blankly for a moment.

'Far as her mother and I knew, she was,' he replied curtly.

'I want all the facts about what happened here this morning,' Pollard told him. 'Repeat, all. I suggest we sit round this table. Please hang on, Inspector Frost. You've the pull over us of getting here first. Now, Mr Gillard, the school bus picks up the Ambercombe children outside the church, doesn't it?'

'That's right,' the farmer replied. He drew the back of his hand across his forehead in a gesture of exhaustion, but had got himself under control. 'Our two board it there, but this morning the boy'd gone ahead on his bike down to Pyrford, to drop in a model aeroplane he'd been working on at a friend's house, and get the bus outside the Stores, so Rosemary was on her own.'

In reply to Pollard's questions it appeared that neither of the Gillard parents had seen Rosemary leave the house. Her father had gone out to the yard at the back before she had finished her breakfast, and her mother, an early riser, was already in the poultry house collecting up the morning's eggs. When Mrs Gillard returned to the kitchen the school bus was just passing the gate, and she had assumed as a matter of course that Rosemary was in it. It was not until half an hour later that she had been startled by the sound of the front door bursting open, and Bill Sandford had rushed in with water dripping from his clothes, to say that he had just got Rosemary out of the quarry pool, and left her wrapped in a blanket in front of the fire in his cottage. The appalled parents had found her semi-conscious, and bleeding from a cut in her head. They rang for an ambulance, and began stripping off her wet clothes. It was then that they found a small packet wrapped in cellophane, fastened inside the top of her tights with a safety pin. While waiting for the ambulance they had opened it.

At this point Inspector Frost broke into Matthew Gillard's narrative to hand Pollard an envelope. Its contents were two pieces of white paper, each of which had been folded and refolded to the smallest possible size, one being much more creased and discoloured than the other.

'The cellophane seems to have kept them dry,' Pollard said, 'but they've been handled so much that there can't be anything in the way of useful dabs, I'm afraid. However, we'll get the forensic people to go over them.'

Toye produced forceps, and the notes were carefully opened out. The paper was of poor quality, and the ink of the ball pen used in each case had run slightly. The messages had been carefully printed in characterless block capitals. The more discoloured and obviously older note read:

NEVER TELL ANYBODY YOU MET ME YESTERDAY OUTSIDE THE CHURCH OR YOU'LL BE TAKEN AWAY FOR GOOD.

The other message was on the same theme:

WHAT HAPPENS TO GIRLS WHO TALK? IT COULD BE YOU NEXT TIME.

There was a violent crash as Matthew Gillard brought his fist down on the table.

'I'd spend the rest o' my life in quod just to get my hands on him ... For Chrissake, can't you get crackin'?'

The telephone rang loudly in the passage leading to the front door, and he made to spring up from his chair.

'Easy,' Pollard said, restraining him. 'We know how you're feeling, but for the moment we're taking any calls.'

An uneasy silence descended. Matthew Gillard breathed heavily, as though he had been running. Toye's voice was faintly audible. His head came round the kitchen door and Pollard was summoned. Going out he braced himself and looked at Toye interrogatively.

'The girl's OK, sir. Shocked, of course, and under treatment, but the head injury was only superficial.'

Releasing a long breath, Pollard strode towards the telephone.

'Tell Gillard,' he said over his shoulder.

A few minutes later he came back to the kitchen.

'Your wife's on the line, Mr Gillard, and would like a word with you.'

Matthew Gillard went out quickly. Pollard propped himself against the kitchen table.

'No hope of seeing Rosemary until tomorrow morning,'

he told the other two. 'They say her condition's satisfactory, but she must be kept quiet, and only the parents allowed in. Your chap's there behind a screen, Frost. Can you send in a relief later? I want anything relevant she says taken down. Meanwhile, we'd better search her room here, Toye, and see Sandford.'

Matthew Gillard reappeared and agreed without demur to having his daughter's bedroom temporarily locked and later searched.

'Take the whole place to pieces if it'll help you get the bastard who wrote those notes,' he said. 'Like me to lend a hand, or would you –'

He broke off at the sound of footsteps in the passage. There was a bang on the kitchen door.

'The Scotland Yard blokes in here?' a man's voice demanded.

'Come in,' Pollard called.

Bill Sandford appeared on the threshold muffled in an old coat, white-faced and taut.

'Come in and welcome,' Matthew Gillard told him. 'There's no paying the debt you're owed here.'

Bill Sandford made a disclamatory gesture, his eyes on Pollard.

'Look here,' he said, 'I don't suppose you'll believe me till you've seen for yourself, but there's a body in the quarry pool.'

Chapter 10

Rain was still falling relentlessly as the five men left Ambercombe Barton for the old quarry in the two police cars,
Pollard, Toye and Inspector Frost in rubber boots and oil-
skins from the Gillards' assortment of wet weather clothing.

Pollard's immediate reaction to Bill Sandford's announce-
ment had been one of scepticism and outrage, but this had
evaporated in seconds. Through long experience of people's
behaviour in crisis situations, he had learnt to recognise
shock. For the moment, at any rate, coat trailing was out,
and past encounters could be conveniently forgotten. He
turned his head and spoke to the occupant of the Hillman's
back seat.

'This body you saw. Did you get the idea that it had been
in the water long?'

'I didn't see it clearly enough to say. It was lying on the
bottom, you see. I –'

'*Lying on the bottom?*'

'Yea.'

Pollard exchanged a lightning glance with Toye. The next
moment the cars came to a halt outside Quarry Cottages.

'Can we all get under cover somewhere, Mr Sandford?
I want you to tell us exactly what happened this morning.'

'Sure. Come into my place.'

They crowded into the living room of the cottage, where
wet clothes were drying in front of the fire, and a damp
patch on the hearthrug showed where the semi-conscious
Rosemary Gillard had been deposited. Bill Sandford indicated his car port facing the front door.

'It was about a quarter to nine. I was just going over to
get some exam scripts which I'd left in the car when I heard
an almighty splash over in the old quarry, and I supposed
a chunk of rock had got loose and fallen into the water. It
happens sometimes. But then I heard a different sort of
splashing – continuous – and belted along to see if a sheep

had fallen over the edge. There's a railing, but it's pretty ropey in places. When I got there I saw it was a person thrashing about, so I kicked my shoes off and went in, yelling that I was coming. Luckily I'm a reasonable swimmer. When I'd taken a few strokes I saw it was young Rosemary. She panicked and struggled a bit, but I managed to get her on my back and grab her wrists, and started off for the side where I'd gone in. It's where the cart track ends, and isn't steep. After I'd been swimming with my legs for a bit, we seemed to be getting there, and I felt with a foot to see if I could touch bottom, and stepped on something that gave in a queer sort of way. I looked down, but I'd churned up muck, and could only see that it was a human body – not any details, I mean. I swam on till I could carry the kid out and cart her along here. You know the rest.'

'You did a damn good job,' Pollard said sincerely, to the accompaniment of gruff inarticulate sounds of assent. 'If you're reasonably warm by now, I'd like to go along and have a look at the place.'

Beyond the cottages the rutted cart track led through a short dark tunnel of trees into the old quarry. Although it was midday, the scene struck Pollard as even more gloomy and derelict than when he had first seen it at nightfall. A sinister note was struck by the continuous appearance and disappearance of countless small circles on the surface of the livid water, giving the impression of some secret activity in progress. He ran his eye over sheer rock faces and abandoned working ledges. On one of these, facing the entrance where he was standing, was a school satchel, tiny, incongruous and pathetic.

'How did she get up there?' he asked Matthew Gillard, who pointed out a steep overgrown path on the right.

'You can get up this way with a bit of a scramble, and about half way round. Far as she got, that is.'

Toye offered to retrieve the satchel and have a look along the ledge. Pollard nodded, and watched him set off up the path.

'If Rosemary went in from where that satchel is, can you work out roughly where you came on the body?' he asked Bill Sandford.

'Very roughly about fifteen feet out from here, I'd say, and about six or eight feet from the rock face on the left.'

Pollard made a quick assessment of these distances and glanced up the almost sheer rock face to the top of the quarry. He saw that at this point the railing had partly collapsed, and that behind it was a thicket of bushes and silver birches. He asked Matthew Gillard if the water level fell much during the summer.

'Not so you'd notice it: not even last summer. It's spring fed, see? Line of springs along the bottom o' the face, over on the left. That's why they didn't work that side much.'

'Want me to rustle up a couple of frogmen?' Inspector Frost asked.

After a brief discussion he went off to ring his head-quarters at Westbridge. As the others waited for Toye to return, Matthew Gillard jerked his head in the direction of the water.

'You think the bloke out there wrote those notes?'

'It depends how long he's been there,' Pollard told him. 'One of the notes was pretty recent, from the look of it. We can't tell till we've got him out. Don't think we're dragging our feet, Mr Gillard. The one thing I'm sure about is that finding the body is an important step forward in a very complicated business.'

Toye rejoined the group, carrying the satchel under a streaming oilskin cape. He reported that the terrace was littered with loose rock fragments.

'Nothing scuffed up. No sign of a struggle at all. No bits of paper or whatever. Half a small footprint that I've covered over as best I can.'

Pollard turned to Matthew Gillard and Bill Sandford.

'I suggest you two go home and get into dry clothes,' he said. 'Inspector Toye and I'll be along later, when we've had a look up at the top there.'

'Reckon you could do with a dry-off yourselves,' the farmer objected. 'Townsfolk aren't used to going around in this sort o' weather. My wife'll be home getting a hot meal, what's more.'

'A good offer we'll be glad to take up soon,' Pollard assured him.

130

The two men went off reluctantly.

'June the eleventh, 1974?' Toye asked, with an upward glance.

'Unless I'm very much mistaken. Let's lock this satchel in the car and scale the heights. Even after nearly eighteen months there could be some handy little telltale trace.'

The path up to the Whitehallow Hills rose steeply behind Quarry Cottages. As he waited for Toye to stow the satchel away in the Hillman, Pollard contemplated Ethel Ridd's cottage. In a curious way, he thought, she herself seemed to be receding into the background as the case developed one fresh complication after another ... The slam of the car door roused him from his thoughts. Toye locked it, and they headed for the path in silence. It was rocky and running with water, shut in on either side by the uncompromisingly straight trunks of spruce fir. High overhead wisps of low cloud wreathed in the treetops. The gradient was taxing to the heavily clothed and booted.

'Good thing we're in reasonable shape,' Pollard remarked, stopping for a breather.

Toye replied that the whole set up was enough to give you the willies, but conceded that it might be a bit better on a fine day. They resumed the climb, and the path suddenly emerged from the claustrophobic conifers into open scrub woodland.

'Guess what!' Pollard exclaimed. 'The downpour's slackening off.'

Astonishingly it was. Overhead the low trailing clouds were breaking up, driven along in a freshening north-west wind, and intermittent scats of rain were replacing the nonstop deluge. As Pollard and Toye came out on to the rounded crest of the Whitehallows ridge there even came a fleeting shaft of pallid sunshine from the south. They were clear of the wooded slopes now, and an expanse of moorland interspersed with outcrops of rock stretched away to the north. Below the crest, and on their right, were the stunted silver birches rising from a thicket which Pollard had noticed from below, behind the gap in the railing. On closer inspection access to the gap seemed impossible without mechanical aids. A huge mass of brambles, about forty feet long and still bearing a few mildewed blackberries, was interlaced with hazel and elder, the whole complex fighting a losing battle with the ivy, which had also begun to throttle the little birch trees. A thriving colony of nettles provided an outer defence at ground level.

'Nobody got a stiff through that lot in June '74,' Toye pronounced.

Pollard agreed. They walked the length of the thicket to test the possibility of getting to the gap along the actual quarry edge. This appeared more practicable from the northern end. By tacit consent he went first. He loathed heights, and it was reassuring to know Toye was at his heels to make an instant grab if necessary. Averting his eyes from the sheer drop and the sullen water below he inched forward on the slippery mud, scanning both ground and bushes. After a back-breaking interval he stopped suddenly, aware of a small tremor of excitement. Some threads were hanging from a tenacious spray of bramble. He disentangled them with infinite care and passed them back to Toye.

'Notice anything?' he asked.

Toye examined the find in silence.

'Two different colours,' he replied at last. 'Brown and white, I'd say.'

'This is it. Old Fatty at North Pyrford said her hiker was wearing a brown and white check shirt, didn't she? However, we'd better not get carried away. Local lads and lasses might come this way in search of cover, though it doesn't seem an ideal spot for fun and games.'

Toye extracted an envelope from an inner pocket, and the threads were put into it and sealed down. The slow progress along the edge of the quarry was resumed, and about ten yards further on they arrived at the gap in the railing. Little trouble appeared to have been taken to put up an effective barrier against venturesome humans or straying animals behind the thicket. Wooden posts supporting a single iron rail lurched at drunken angles and were rotten with damp. Here two lay on the ground, having brought the rail down with them.

'A push would have done it easily,' Pollard said, inspect-

132

ing the posts. 'Here, watch out, for God's sake!'

Toye was craning over the edge, and reported that they seemed right over the spot where, according to Mr Sandford, the body would have hit the water.

They made a painstaking search of the ground and bushes behind the gap but found nothing suggestive of human activity.

'It's these bloody brambles and things being so tough,' Pollard said at last. 'You could roll half a dozen corpses about without snapping bits off. We'd better pack it in.'

They began to work back to their point of entry, giving every inch of the way a second scrutiny. Suddenly the sun came out, and simultaneously Toye called a halt.

'There's a bit of white paper stuck in the middle of these brambles,' he said. 'Torn off something. It just caught my eye with the sun on it ... Ouch!'

'Take off that cape thing and wrap it round your hand,' Pollard advised. 'The Gillards can put in a claim if it gets torn.'

The fragment of paper was damp, but Toye managed to extract it undamaged. In itself it was disappointing: the torn-off corner of a printed page. The number, 44, was just distinguishable, and there were traces of the opening words of several lines.

'It must have come from somebody who went along here,' Pollard said, staring at it. 'I can't believe that it got blown up from the quarry and landed in that bush ... Poorish paper. Looks like a bit of a cheap magazine or a paperback. We'll get the lab people to have a go.'

Nothing further came to light, and they were soon on their way down to Quarry Cottages, drying off as they went. Bill Sandford raised a hand in greeting as they passed his window and reached their car. In under five minutes they were at Ambercombe Barton. Margaret Gillard, looking strained and acutely unhappy, whisked a dish of lamb chops and potatoes on to the table, and urged them to get something inside them. Her husband had gone to the hospital, she told them, and she herself was driving over again when he came back.

'I'll never forgive myself,' she burst out suddenly. 'Being

so sharp and bustling the child along, and all the time she was scared out of her wits.'

Pollard attempted what he felt was very inadequate reassurance. He learnt that Rosemary had not referred to the notes, and in accordance with his orders no one had mentioned them to her.

'She knows a policewoman's there,' Margaret Gillard said dully, depositing an apple pie and a pot of tea on the table. 'She seems glad. It makes her feel safer, I suppose.'

Just as Pollard and Toye were finishing their meal a call came through from Inspector Frost. Two naval frogmen with the necessary equipment and an ambulance were shortly leaving for Ambercombe. He himself would come along with a constable to keep any locals from making nuisances of themselves. Returning to the kitchen Pollard passed on this information, and asked if he and Toye could have a look at Rosemary's bedroom in the meantime. Margaret Gillard led the way upstairs to a pleasant little room, abruptly burst into tears, and left them to it. Pollard looked around. The wallpaper sprigged with rosebuds and the dainty pink and white of curtains and quilt suggested a conventional mother's, rather than a contemporary teenager's ideas of bedroom décor. He inspected the books on a shelf, and found them childish for a girl of fifteen, and the pictures on the walls equally so. Only a couple of small pinups of current pop idols in a dark corner, and a few with-it magazines on the windowsill indicated a tentative attempt on Rosemary's part to identify with her generation. Almost completely alienated from her mother, he thought, and he wondered about Matthew Gillard as a father. Too down-to-earth and inarticulate, perhaps, however devoted underneath. The prospect of the twins' adolescent years suddenly loomed up ominously, but the thought of Jane in the background was reassuring.

A search of the chest of drawers and wardrobe uncovered a pathetic little cache of cheap cosmetics, but nothing connected with the threatening notes. They stripped the bed and discovered a slit in the mattress cover, inside which was a packet of newspaper cuttings relating to kidnappings and rapes of young girls. The really significant thing, they both agreed, was the blacking out of 11 June in the 1975 calendar on the wall.

'I'm prepared to bet,' Pollard said, flicking over the tabs for the other months, 'that she met the hiker on that day in '74, and the chap we're after found out. How, I wonder? Everything depends on what I can get from her tomorrow. And why wasn't she at school? It was a Tuesday, and they'd have had the Whitsun break, surely?'

They went downstairs and found Margaret Gillard feverishly attacking household chores.

'The day Mr Viney died?' she said, breaking off to answer Pollard's question. 'Yes, Rosemary'd been away from school with the mumps all the week before. I remember she started again the next morning.'

She looked at Pollard with a puzzled expression, but the sound of cars arriving broke off the conversation. An ambulance, a small van with two naval frogmen and their gear, and a police car bringing Inspector Frost and a constable indicated that the enquiry into Ethel Ridd's murder was about to move into a further and grimmer phase.

As Pollard expected it soon became clear that the news of Bill Sandford's discovery had leaked out. During the frogmen's preparations at the old quarry local people began to gravitate to the scene, their curiosity aroused by the convoy of official vehicles. It was not long before a couple of newsmen appeared, armed with cameras. Pollard had already decided that as the threatening notes were now in the hands of the police, Rosemary Gillard was no longer in danger from their writer. The best policy now was to rattle him by giving them maximum publicity. In reply to a barrage of questions, he stated their contents, and gave the details of Rosemary Gillard's attempted suicide and her rescue by Bill Sandford, adding that a further development was imminent. This handout was received with vociferous gratitude, one of the newsmen haring to the Ambercombe call box, while the other hastily photographed Bill Sandford in conference with the frogmen, while hovering for an opportunity to interview him. Meanwhile the crowd of onlookers grew rapidly, but was firmly kept back by the Westbridge police.

135

Once started, operations moved rapidly. A searchlight was directed onto the water at a spot indicated by Bill Sandford. One of the frogmen entered the water, submerged, and a couple of moments later reappeared, indicating that the beam of light should be moved slightly to the left. He emerged to report that the body on the bottom was weighted down by a rucksack full of stones. There was a tense interval during which this was detached and brought out, slimy, dripping and weed-encrusted. Pollard and Toye superintended its envelopment in polythene sheeting and transfer to the van. A tense hush descended on the waiting crowd at the entrance to the quarry. The ambulance manoeuvred forward, blocking the view and causing some murmurs of indignation, and a stretcher was taken to the water's edge. Finally the frogmen brought out their nightmare burden, which was hurriedly covered and hustled into the ambulance as the newsmen's cameras clicked from the nearest sanctioned vantage point, and Inspector Frost cleared a passage through the onlookers.

The underwater investigations continued. Pollard and Toye, who had exchanged a quick triumphant glance at the sight of a disintegrating brown and white check shirt as the body was brought out of the water, waited hopefully. The frogmen submerged again to search the bottom of the quarry pool. In a relatively short time a pair of heavy walking shoes packed with stones was brought to the surface. Finally and unexpectedly a gun was found embedded in the bed.

'A Colt ·38,' Pollard said, examining it. 'We'll get it cleaned up, but I don't think the serial number's likely to be on the police list of legally owned firearms in these parts.'

The return to Westbridge was followed by intense activity. An urgent post-mortem on the body was arranged. Preliminary forensic tests on the rucksack, the remains of the shirt and the threads found in the thicket were put in hand. The mud and weeds encrusting the shoes were carefully removed, preparatory to identifying the make of the latter. Pollard reported briefly to his Assistant Commissioner's office, and held a press conference at which he succeeded in being wholly non-committal on the possible connection between Ethel Ridd's murder and that of the man found in the quarry pool. Finally he rang the hospital, and learnt to his relief that Rosemary Gillard's condition was satisfactory, and that he would be able to see her on the following morning. These matters having been attended to he sat down to a hasty meal with Toye. For a time they ate in silence.

'Frenzied activity without progress,' Pollard suddenly remarked.

'I wouldn't say that,' Toye replied. 'Your hunch that it was blurting out about the hiker and not the chalice that did for Ethel Ridd has paid off all along the line. The chap must've been a threat to somebody in the place. Once we get him identified we'll be more or less home and dry.'

'My next hunch is that it's not going to be all that easy to get him identified. Remember that the Missing Persons Register didn't help? And it's going to be one hell of a job to prove where local people were all that time ago.'

'Thinking of George Aldridge?' Toye asked.

'Yea. I can see him now sitting in that pretentious back room office of his, sweating like a pig. Let's go and look up your notes.'

They returned to their room at Westbridge police station and spent some time discussing the record of their interviews with the two Aldridges, finally making out a timetable of George's alleged movements on the afternoon of Wednesday 19 November:

1.30 p.m. Leaves fruit depot at Marchester. (Salesman's evidence.)
2.00 p.m. G.A. claims to have left depot.
2.30 p.m. G.A. claims to have arrived in Pyrford.
2.50 p.m. Arrives in Pyrford. (Martha Rook's evidence.)
3.00 p.m. Snip van arrives. (Martha Rook's evidence.) Aldridge's van driven into yard and doors closed.
3.45–6.00 p.m. Stores checked and put away. (Statement made by both Aldridges.)
6.00 p.m. Shop closed. (Martha Rook's evidence.)
6.30 p.m. Aldridges' supper. (Statement by G.A.)

'So what?' Pollard remarked, after studying the document

137

critically. 'Aldridge is a liar, of course, and a fairly incompetent one at that. He couldn't have got back to Pyrford from the centre of Marchester in half an hour, to start with. He's got a good half-hour not accounted for. Pity the Marchester chaps don't seem able to pick up his trail after leaving the depot. Then there's a good deal of this that hangs on Martha Rook's unsupported statements. Personally I shouldn't think she'd miss a trick, but she surely can't have sat glued to her window from one o'clock to an unspecified time after the bus from Marchester decanted her pals at half past six. What about going to the loo then making a cup of tea? We'd better see her again, and risk her talking and putting Aldridge on his guard. And the Snip driver, too. Was Aldridge really there all through the delivery of the stores?'

Toye agreed that these enquiries ought to be made.

'Trouble is the timing, as we've seen all along. We accept that Aldridge couldn't have got to Ambercombe *before* Ridd. Martha Rook's definite that he drove into Pyrford in his own van at 2.45 or a shade later. I can't believe he could have driven it up to Ambercombe while Snip was delivering stock without her noticing, let alone murdered Ridd and got back again within the hour, to put it away in his yard just after 3.45, as Martha Rook says he did.'

'Neither can I,' Pollard said, leaning back in his chair and frowning in the effort of concentration, 'quite apart from sitting on the vicarage stairs with half a brick until Ridd conveniently turned up. The later time, after Snip had gone, is slightly less improbable, but there we're up against the unlikelihood of Ridd leaving the locking-up until it was close on dark, and how the hell could he have known that she was going to, anyway? It's not a cast iron alibi, but not far short of one. I'm banking everything on getting some definite lead out of Rosemary Gillard tomorrow morning. By the way, we might look through her satchel while we're waiting to hear something from the pathologist bloke doing the P-M.'

They examined the contents of the satchel thoroughly, but found no direct reference to the events behind the notes. Pollard was interested in various items in a rough note book.

There were a number of names and obviously fictitious addresses in remote parts of the world. A series of drawings showed a figure of indeterminate sex escaping from a prowling beast. Wish-fulfilment symbols, poor kid, he thought. He glanced through exercise books. The work in them showed intelligence but was wildly variable in standard, as frequent comments in red emphasised with asperity.

Later a preliminary report came through from the pathologist.

'The chap was between forty-five and fifty-five,' Pollard told Toye on ringing off. 'He was about five foot eight and rather lightly built. Shot in the back of the head and dead before going into the water, somewhere between fifteen and twenty months ago. We'll get more details tomorrow morning.'

Chapter 11

'We've got the bullet out,' the pathologist told Pollard on the following morning. 'It's ·38 calibre and in fair condition, but whether you'll be able to prove it came from the gun is another matter.'

'We'll have a go,' Pollard replied. 'Incidentally, no certificate's been issued for the Colt. Now that you've had a bit longer on the job, are you able to narrow down the probable date of death at all?'

'You're all the same, you chaps, wherever you come from,' grumbled the pathologist. 'Land us with these foul jobs and expect the impossible. I'm sticking to what I said last night, but unofficially I'll add a rider that the earlier date – twenty months ago – seems slightly more probable than the later one. I'll let you have the dental details and exact measurements, and my final estimate of his age by lunchtime.'

Pollard thanked him and went off for his vital interview with Rosemary Gillard. To his relief the ward sister was welcoming and co-operative.

'Physically there's nothing wrong with Rosemary,' she told him over a cup of coffee in her office. 'She's not what I call a robust type, but normally healthy. What her psychological state is after all she's been through, I can't say, of course. Mr Lindsey, our senior psychiatrist, hasn't seen her yet.'

'And she hasn't referred either to the notes or to her attempted suicide?' Pollard asked.

'Not to the notes. She asked the policewoman last night if she would get into trouble over what she did in the quarry, but didn't follow it up. She was reassured, of course, and told not to worry about it at all.'

'What do you make of her yourself?' Pollard asked.

'It's not easy to make anything much of her at the moment,' Sister Penrose replied frankly. 'She's driven right in on herself. She strikes me as intelligent, but childish for a girl of fifteen these days. The mother's the energetic dominating sort, and the father's inarticulate. Mind you, they're devoted to her. This business has knocked them for six. But there's no real contact – not at present. It's partly the generation gap, of course. She just couldn't talk to them about those notes.'

'Well, wish me luck, Sister,' Pollard said. 'Somehow or other I've got to get her to talk to me.'

His first impression of Rosemary Gillard on this occasion was of big anxious brown eyes, too large for a pale face with fine-drawn features. She was sitting up in bed in a small side ward, wearing a pink knitted jacket trimmed with bows of ribbon. The little room was gay with flowers. A bowl of fruit and a box of sweets were on her locker, and a scatter of magazines lay unread on the quilt.

'Here's such a famous visitor to see you, Rosemary,' Sister Penrose told her, 'Detective-Superintendent Pollard from Scotland Yard. Aren't you the lucky one?'

Rosemary Gillard gave a forced little smile, and her eyes followed her exit uneasily. Pollard sat down in the visitor's chair by the bed and produced a gaily wrapped parcel from his coat pocket.

'I guessed you'd have lots of flowers,' he said, 'and I know that a good many young ladies are figure-conscious these days, so I kept off chocolates.'

He put the parcel on the bed. Her thanks were barely audible, but on extracting bath salts elegantly packaged she coloured with pleasure. Pollard sensed that classifying her as a young lady had struck the right note. Then she abruptly put the gift down and looked at him challengingly.

'Why are people sending me flowers and giving me presents? I did a dreadful wicked thing.'

Her voice quivered into silence.

'No,' Pollard replied, 'you've got it wrong, Rosemary. What you did was very nearly to make a bad mistake. The flowers and presents are to tell you how glad people are that it didn't come off. I know that I am. You see, I'll never be able to find out who killed poor Ethel Ridd without your help.'

She stared at him.

'But – but it must've been that awful man.'

'You mean the man you met on the morning of June the eleventh last year, the day old Mr Viney died?' Pollard asked, deciding to take a chance.

To his relief she nodded dumbly.

'Listen,' he said, 'what I want you to do is to think back to that morning, Rosemary, and tell me absolutely everything you can remember about the man. I mean exactly what he looked like and said to you, and where and when you met him.'

She gave a convulsive shudder and buried her face in her hands.

'Oh, don't make me, please don't! I don't want to remember him. I can't get to sleep night-times for thinking he'll come and get me, like he said in those notes.'

'But how could he?' Pollard asked, deliberately matter-of-fact. 'He's dead.'

He saw her hands drop from her face, and a sudden transfiguring expression of relief turn to one of unwilling incredulity.

'Dead? You're sure it's him?' she asked breathlessly.

'Quite sure, Rosemary. After he met you he met somebody else. This person shot him, and threw him over the edge of the quarry into the water. Was he carrying a pack on his back when you met him?'

Looking stunned, she nodded assent.

'Whoever shot him left the pack on him, but took everything out and then filled it up with stones so that the body couldn't float. Mr Sandford found it on the bottom when he rescued you yesterday. So you don't have to think about him any more, do you?'

Pollard watched her trying to make some sense out of the facts he had given her.

'But if he was killed the morning I saw him, who was it wrote and said he'd come and take me away if I let on?' she burst out, gripped by her fears once again.

'I'm sure you can work that one out, Rosemary,' Pollard told her, and waited with interest.

'The – the *other* man? The one who killed the man I saw?'

'Quite right. Let's call him X, shall we, like the number you have to find out in algebra problems? We know that the man who talked to you came down from the path along the top of the Whitehallows, and wasn't likely to have met any Ambercombe people. X was banking on nobody having seen him, so that no awkward questions would be asked when he disappeared. We don't know how X found out that he'd talked to you: perhaps the man mentioned it. At any rate, X decided that you'd got to be kept quiet. Now do you see how Miss Ridd comes in?'

'She – she said a hiker had come into the church during the service, didn't she?'

'Yes. In the Consistory Court in Marchester, in front of a lot of people. So X decided that he'd got to make sure she couldn't tell anybody any more about the man, and he made sure, that same day.'

Better to let her work things out herself, Pollard thought, as a lengthy silence built up, and fear and unhappiness crept back into Rosemary's face.

'But you haven't caught X,' she said piteously at last. 'He could still come ...'

'Nonsense!' Pollard replied robustly. 'That's not nearly up to your usual standard, as schoolteachers say. You've been very quick to cotton on up to now. As soon as X knows that we know that you saw the man he killed, there won't be any point in trying to keep you quiet about it, will there? Too late for that now: we're closing in on him. All right? Any more questions?'

'How will he find out?' she persisted.

Pollard smiled at her.

'Downstairs,' he said, 'newspaper men and chaps from broadcasting are lying in wait for me. I'll see you get today's *Westbridge Evening News* ... Now then, Miss Gillard, about this help you're going to give me. To start with, you'd been ill, hadn't you, and that was why you were at home on a schoolday?'

In the relief of miraculous deliverance from her long nightmare Rosemary Gillard poured out her story. Yes, she had been off school all the week before with the mumps. The swelling hadn't gone down till the Monday, and her

143

mother thought she had better stay home one more day to make sure. It was a lovely morning, real summer, and she had gone over to a farm on the far side of Ambercombe village with a message. On her way back she saw a hiker standing by the church gate and looking up and down the road. She knew he was a hiker because of his clothes: dirty old jeans, light-coloured ones, and a shirt with big brown and white checks open at the neck. He wanted a shave, too, and had a rucksack on his back, and dusty shoes. He had watched her coming along and spoken to her.

'What did he say?' Pollard asked.

'Hiya, little English rose!' Rosemary replied, colouring slightly with embarrassment.

'Was he a foreigner, then?'

'Well, he sounded just a bit like an American on the telly. Not much though – you know.'

The man had asked her name and said it suited her, but seemed more interested in who lived at the Barton, saying it was a fine old house, and surprised to learn that it was her father's farm. Then he'd said Ambercombe was a tiny little place and he supposed most people lived at Pyrford, the village he'd seen from the top of the hill. She had answered that they did. The shop was down there, and the inn, and there were quite a lot of houses. Realising that time was getting on, she had told him that she must go home and help her mother with the dinner, and added she hoped he would enjoy the rest of his hike. Then he had suddenly looked dreadful, and she'd felt scared.

'Can you explain just how he looked dreadful?' Pollard asked her, and learned that the man's mouth had gone all tight, and he'd glared at her and said he was out for a lot more than a hike. She had hurried off home without looking back, but on reaching the gate of the Barton glanced quickly over her shoulder, and saw the man going away up the road. When she got into the kitchen it was twenty past eleven. She noticed the time as her mother remarked that she hadn't hurried herself, and had better get on with the potatoes.

Pollard sat in silent satisfaction for a few moments. Not only had he managed to handle Rosemary Gillard with a success beyond his hopes, but her description of the hiker and the timing of their encounter fitted Clara Hayball's evidence with remarkable accuracy. Moreover the man's interest in local residents and final remark could reasonably be taken to point to a pre-arranged interview – fixed over the telephone call from North Pyrford, probably – which was likely to be stormy. He surfaced as Rosemary rather shyly ventured a remark.

'I do remember one other thing about him,' she volunteered. 'He'd got a book in his hand.'

'What sort of book?'

'Quite a small one in paper covers. I expect it was a guide book: hikers coming this way often have them – you know.'

Pollard made a mental note that this additional piece of information could tie up with the torn scrap of a printed page found in the bush above the quarry. If it was from a local guide book, which seemed quite credible, it should be possible to check up on the book's purchase somewhere in the district.

'You've helped me tremendously, Rosemary,' he told her. 'You're very observant and you've got a good memory. Let's go on to those two notes that X wrote to keep you quiet about having seen the hiker. Were there any others?'

Rosemary shook her head.

'How soon did the first one come?'

'The next morning, when I went back to school I – I thought the man was playing a joke on me at first. Then I remembered how he'd changed all of a sudden, and I felt scared, because he'd found out all about me – about me going in the school bus, I mean.'

'The school bus?' Pollard echoed, mystified for the moment.

'Yes. The note had been put in the bus. Dropped through a window, Jeff said. They don't all shut properly – it's an awful old boneshaker.'

By dint of further questions Pollard managed to get the facts clear. The school bus was operated by the joint owners of the Pyrford Garage, either one of whom did the two daily runs into Westbridge in term time. When not on the road the bus stood in the lay-by next to the garage. On the morning of

145

12 June Jeff Thomas, one of the garage owners, had noticed an envelope addressed to Rosemary Gillard lying on a seat, and had handed it to her when she boarded the bus at Ambercombe. There had been a good deal of teasing on the way into Westbridge, everyone assuming that the note was from a boy ...

As he listened to Rosemary's disjointed narrative Pollard had a clear mental picture of the lie of the land in relation to the Pyrford Garage. Just beyond it he had watched the school bus manoeuvring into the lay-by on the previous morning, as he and Toye had been held up in the rain on the way to North Pyrford. On the opposite side of the road into Pyrford village, and almost facing the garage was the Village Stores, with its second entrance through the yard. What could be simpler for slipping out late at night, after the garage had closed and the traffic on the main road had died down? Especially, he thought, if you had a wife like Mrs Aldridge with an unshakable determination not to be involved. He took a firm hold on his mounting sense of excitement at this pointer, and asked about the second note. This, she told him, had been put in the bus, too, and given to her on Wednesday morning. The immediate outcome of his television appeal on Tuesday evening for information about the hiker, Pollard reflected.

After a few minutes of personal chat with Rosemary, aimed at helping her on her way back to a normal existence, he left her with a parting wave from the door. On the way through the main ward he got an interrogative glance from Sister Penrose, in attendance on something very exalted in the consultant line. He returned a discreet V-sign, and headed for the outer world and the police station. However, by the time he had given Toye the gist of Rosemary Gillard's story, the amount of ground still to be covered, if a double murder charge was ever to be brought against Aldridge, was appearing decidedly daunting.

'Let's face it,' he said, tilting his chair back and frowning heavily. 'We haven't a clue about what Aldridge was doing on the morning of June the eleventh last year, and finding out is going to be the devil. At the moment he's got what looks like a convincing alibi for Ridd's murder. We know

146

absolutely nothing about any link between him and a stranger to the place with an American accent. On the other hand he's lying about his movements after leaving the court on November the nineteenth. He was scared stiff when we talked to him. He's a local, and would know all about Rosemary Gillard, and could easily have slipped out and dropped notes into the school bus on both occasions. Where do we go from here, for heaven's sake? Or are we barking up the wrong tree altogether? If so, how do we find the right one? What goes on?' he added rather irritably, aware of constant comings and goings in the corridor. 'There seems to be a good bit of activity.'

'A chap said they'd brought in a bloke wanted for selling stuff from hijacked lorries,' Toye told him.

As he spoke steps halted outside the door which opened to admit Inspector Frost's head.

'Glad you're in,' he said, entering and shutting the door behind him. 'It mayn't be worth anything to you, but we've picked up the chap from the Pyrford shop. Aldridge is the name. In with a racket selling stuff from hijacked lorries,' he added, gratified by the effect of his news.

Pollard brought his hand down on the table with a stifled exclamation.

'Let's have the details.'

It appeared that the Marchester and Westbridge police had known for some time that a racket was operating in the area for the sale of goods from lorries hijacked in other parts of the country. Vans bearing fictitious names were making contact with buyers. A number of shopkeepers in a relatively small way of business were being kept under observation. Early that morning a Westbridge patrol car had intercepted a suspicious van, and brought it in with its driver on whom a list of the day's rendezvous had been found. One of these had been for 10 a.m., at a spot described as 'quarry on main road two miles north of Pyrford opposite field gate.' A discreet watch had been kept by plain clothes men in unofficial cars, and just before ten the Pyrford Village Stores van had come along and turned into the quarry. The police cars had promptly driven up and blocked the exit.

'Just the place for a spot of funny business,' Frost said.

'It's another of these disused quarries, like the Ambercombe one, only dry. Plenty of room for several cars: I've seen people camping there in the summer. Aldridge started off by blustering and talking about his rights, of course. Said he was simply picking up some lines cheap from a chap who bought up damaged stuff after warehouse fires, and had come along to save him the bother of coming on to Pyrford. Just the guff you'd expect. We took him back to his place, and there were a lot of cigarettes and tinned meat and bottles of gin and whisky he couldn't produce invoices or receipts for. So he's here – helping the police with their enquiries. And where we thought you people might come in was that when we brought 'em together they went for each other hell for leather. The driver chap accused Aldridge of grassing on him because of a row they'd had last Wednesday week about a case of whisky being a couple of bottles short. You weren't satisfied about Aldridge's account of his movements that afternoon, if I remember rightly?'

'We were not. Because he was obviously lying about his return from Marchester after lunch: we've been wondering all along if his alibi for the Ridd murder was bustable after all. This business you've uncovered accounts for the lies, and also for his alarm at being questioned by us. He's inflated with self-importance, and if it came out that he'd been dealing in stolen goods, what price his local standing – being a churchwarden and whatever?'

'Like to have a word with him yourself?' Frost suggested.

'If you're through with him for the moment, yes,' Pollard replied unenthusiastically, getting to his feet and giving Toye a glance indicating the end of the road.

At Frost's order a constable posted outside a door admitted them to a small room furnished with a battered wooden table and four hard upright chairs. The walls were a stained and faded green and the window was high and inaccessible. An unshaded electric light-bulb was switched on. George Aldridge, sleek black hair disordered and shirt collar askew, was slumped at the table. A tray with an untouched cup of tea and a plate of sandwiches had been pushed aside. As Pollard and Toye came in he swung round at them like a cornered animal.

148

'They've no bloody right to keep me here, they haven't,' he said furiously, his normally careful speech going to the winds. 'How the hell was I to know the stuff that bleeder offered me'd been pinched? Sent for my solicitor, I 'ave.'

Pollard sat down facing him. Toye took another chair. There was a brief silence.

'You're a fool, Aldridge,' Pollard remarked dispassionately. 'Can't you see that it's in your own interest to prove beyond doubt that you were taking in stuff in that quarry not long before you turned up at your shop just in time for the Snip delivery on the afternoon of November the nineteenth? You'd come the long way round from Marchester, hadn't you, in case you were noticed driving past the turning into the village on the way to the quarry?'

George Aldridge gaped and stared, his little black eyes seeming to recede into his white pasty face.

'Inspector Toye and I couldn't care less about your commercial activities,' Pollard went on. 'Our business' – he leant forward and spoke slowly and deliberately – 'is to find out in the first place who killed Ethel Ridd that afternoon. If you can prove that you were late getting home from Marchester because you came the long way round to meet a chap in that quarry, well, you couldn't have been the killer, could you? We have a witness that the Snip van arrived just after you, and that when it left again at a quarter to four you put your own van away in your yard and shut the door.'

George Aldridge gave a strangled yelp and gripped the edge of the table.

'So now you're trying to fix Ridd's murder on me too, are you? I tell you I can prove I was up to the quarry before I got 'ome. Ask 'im – the bastard that's been selling me stolen stuff, an' cases o' whisky with bottles short. Ask Redshaw. 'E went by in 'is car, and saw me an' the van. Came into the Stores next day, gave me a wink, blast 'im, sayin' 'e wouldn't give a pal away. Police can find 'im in New York, can't they, if they want to? Or was it 'im that grassed on me after all?'

The agitated appeal faded into a dead silence. As Pollard surfaced voices were audible in the corridor, and Inspector

Frost came in to inform George Aldridge that his solicitor had arrived.

Pollard and Toye extricated themselves and made for their own quarters. Sinking on to a chair, Pollard took out a handkerchief and mopped his brow.

'Redshaw,' he said at last. 'So he'd have got home soon after half past two, not at five o'clock.'

'Not at five o'clock,' Toye echoed, 'just as the ruddy church clock was striking.'

'What in hell have we missed out on? But I'll tell you one thing, Toye. Whatever it is, the urgent thing now is to find out for sure if Redshaw really has gone to New York and when he's expected back. If he suddenly turns up and hears what's happened to Aldridge, what price a third murder after all? Aldridge will be bailed, of course ... Pyrford right away, don't you think?'

While on the now familiar road they decided to make a preliminary call at the Rectory.

'Even if Hoyle doesn't know when Redshaw's due back here,' Pollard said, 'he'll be able to put us in touch with whatever domestic help they do have, who is sure to know more or less.'

In reply to their ring the door was flung open so swiftly that a caller had obviously been expected. Robert Hoyle looked momentarily astonished.

'Do come in,' he said, leading the way to his study. 'As a matter of fact I'm expecting Inspector Frost. He rang to say that he'd be looking in. Sit down, won't you? I expect you've heard about this latest trouble of ours, right on the heels of poor little Rosemary Gillard's affair yesterday.'

'If it's the George Aldridge business, yes, we do know about it,' Pollard told him. 'We happened to be at the West-bridge police station when they brought him in with the other chap. We'd like to say how sorry we are about this run of disasters, padre, especially for you personally.'

'That's kind of you. Life does seem a bit much at the moment, Aldridge being my senior churchwarden. I suppose there's no doubt that he's been involved with this stolen goods racket?'

'Absolutely none, I should think. He was caught red-

150

handed. Of course he'll swear he didn't know the stuff had been pinched, but I shouldn't think he'll get away with it.'

Robert Hoyle groaned.

'The awful part is that quite a lot of people in the parish will be quite pleased about it in a thoroughly uncharitable way. He's not at all liked, you know. Always throwing his weight about. I can't see how he can go on being church-warden ... However, I mustn't inflict my troubles on you: you've plenty of problems of your own. Can I be of any use?'

'We just called in to ask if you knew when Mr Redshaw will be getting back,' Pollard replied. 'We want to check a point of timing with him, and hear he's gone to New York. To be honest we didn't want to spend time getting involved with Mrs Redshaw.'

For a moment Robert Hoyle looked amused and less care-worn.

'You'd have been quite safe: she went off with him early yesterday morning. He's attending some literary dinner over there, and they thought they might have a short holiday while they were about it, possibly flying down to Florida for a few days. Wouldn't it be terrific to be able to whisk one's wife off for a break like that?' he added wistfully.

'Terrific,' Pollard agreed. 'I'd like to do it right now. So there's no firm date for their return?'

'Not as far as I know. I expect they'll let their daily woman know. She's a Mrs Tucker: her cottage is the first on the right down Church Lane.'

Feeling relieved at the Redshaws' absence, Pollard kept the conversation going for a few minutes before thanking Robert Hoyle and saying that they must push on.

'That's a bit of luck,' he remarked to Toye when the Rectory door had closed behind them. 'Redshaw being out of the way before Aldridge was pulled in, I mean. It's most unlikely to get into any English paper that he'll see. But I'm contacting the Yard at once. The FBI must be asked to keep an eye on him, and let us know at once if he makes a sudden break for home.'

'Don't you think the business of Rosemary Gillard and the notes may get quite a bit of press coverage?' Toye asked.

151

'It's possible, but I don't for a moment think that would bring him back. Too late to bump her off now.'

They drove into the village and parked by the call box in which Pollard was incarcerated for some time. He finally emerged to report that things were under control, and asked what was happening at the shop.

'Business is brisk,' Toye reported. 'Mrs Aldridge seems to be coping all right.'

'Do you know, I wouldn't be surprised if she doesn't see a chance of cutting loose from him ... We'd better make for that farm where Redshaw said he collected a couple of ambrosial ducks on the way back from Marchester. The time should fit in with when he passed Aldridge at the quarry.'

Reference to the file and an ordnance map located Breakacres Farm at about a mile north of the turning to North Pyrford.

'Let's work out times,' Pollard said. 'Martha Rook said Aldridge drove into Pyrford at "turned ten to three". He had to start back from the quarry about twenty to three, I should think. If Redshaw collected the ducks not long before half past two, it would fit. Let's go.'

'Do you think Mrs Redshaw was lying about the time he got home?' Toye asked, as they emerged on to the main road and headed north.

'I don't know. I didn't think so when we saw her. She's the vague, woolly sort, of course. What's more puzzling is why Martha Rook *didn't* see him coming in just before Aldridge, and *did* at five. What did he do with his car in the meantime? I suppose she could have made a mistake. We'd better see her again.'

Breakacres Farm was located without difficulty. A board outside a gate announced that poultry, cream and free range eggs were obtainable. The gate opened on to a farm track, the house itself being some distance from the main road. Toye commented unfavourably, and negotiated the track with care. As the Hillman approached the cluster of farm buildings an assortment of dogs materialised noisily, bringing an elderly woman in a bright flowered overall to a door. The older generation of farmer's wife, Pollard thought, noting the straight grey hair swept back into a bun, the thick woollen stockings and stout low-heeled shoes, and contrasting her with Margaret Gillard. The dogs subsided, and he got out of the car.

'Good afternoon,' he said pleasantly. 'A friend of mine, Mr Redshaw of Pyrford, told me your ducks are simply delicious. I wonder if I could have one?'

The woman looked distressed.

'I'm sorry, sir, but I haven't a single bird ready dressed. Tell the truth, we don't reckon to get casual customers this time of year: only our regulars.'

Pollard expressed disappointment.

'I ought to have rung you, Mrs – Mrs?'

'Darch, sir.'

'Mrs Darch. I expect Mr Redshaw did last week?'

'That's right, sir. He rang the Tuesday morning, and said he'd come the long way round from Marchester Wednesday, and pick 'em up. So I put a couple of lovely birds down in the box by the gate before dinner, to save him coming all the way up here. They has an account, you see – pays monthly.'

After admiring the farmhouse, and assuring Mrs Darch that he would order in advance on his next visit to the area, Pollard returned to the car.

'No joy,' he reported. 'The ducks were dumped in that mail box down by the gate at dinner time for Redshaw to pick up. I think we'd better run over to Marchester, and ask them to help find out what he really did after coming out of the Chapter House.'

Toye drew up at the gate and enquired which route they should take.

'Which will get us there soonest?'

'Back past Pyrford. It's a bit longer from here, but a much faster road.'

'OK. Past Pyrford, then. How I'm beginning to hate the sight of the place.'

Traffic was light, and Toye kept up a steady fifty until obliged to reduce speed on the outskirts of the village.

'Can you beat it?' he exclaimed indignantly. 'There's that ruddy bus holding everybody up again! Why didn't the chap turn the thing when he got back this morning, same as yesterday?'

He braked as the school bus waited for a north-bound lorry before emerging from the gateway into which it had backed. As it set off on its afternoon run to Westbridge, Toye let in the clutch and the Hillman began to move.

'Stop!' Pollard shouted. 'Pull into the lay-by.'

Toye hastily complied and turned to him in astonishment.

'Do you see what I see now the bloody bus has gone?' Pollard demanded. 'That open gate's the end of a lane. It doesn't lead into a field at all.'

The next moment they were out of the car, the training of years compelling Toye to pause to lock it before following on. The lane was narrow and rough, rising fairly steeply and bearing right. They walked round the curve and found themselves confronting the palatial garage of the Old Rectory which they had admired from above. Beyond it a branch of the drive ran up steeply to join the main approach to the house. For a moment they were silent.

'I see how it was done now,' Pollard said. 'Redshaw came on here, perhaps dawdling for the last bit till the main road was clear and he could turn up this lane unnoticed, and leave his car out of sight at the bend. Then he went through the garden at the back of the house, and up through the woods to Ambercombe on foot. He could easily have got to the vicarage by half past three, and found it was still open. He went in and waited. Perhaps he meant to strangle Ridd, and then changed his mind when he noticed that loose brick in the kitchen. Having done the job he came back the same way, and backed the car in neutral down to the road. There was a risk in starting up the engine so near the Pyrford Garage: it might have attracted attention. In his place I think I'd have waited for a passing car to drown the sound. All he had to do then was to drive carefully round the corner into Martha Rook's field of vision, and turn left for home. He took colossal risks, but one's got to remember that he had to improvise the entire plan between Ethel Ridd's exit from the Chapter House, and one o'clock when the court

154

rose ... Bit of luck for us that you decided to take this road, old man.'

He lifted an eyebrow at Toye who promptly disclaimed any credit, saying that it was spotting the lane and seeing what it added up to that had brought home the bacon.

'What it hasn't brought home, unfortunately, is why Redshaw had to murder the hiker in the first place,' Pollard reminded him. 'Obviously the chap was such a threat to him that he couldn't see any other way out. The next job is digging into Redshaw's past. We'll go up tonight and get a Yard team going on it, taking the P-M report and all the bits and pieces. Back to Westbridge first, though, to put them in the picture.'

Chapter 12

On Pollard and Toye's return to Westbridge there was a hastily convened conference with the Chief Constable, Superintendent Canning and Inspector Frost. Pollard's account of the day's events created a minor sensation.

'I'd stake my pension that Redshaw committed both murders,' he concluded, 'but of course we're not even within shouting distance of bringing a charge.'

'I suppose the hiker chap unwisely tried to blackmail him,' Colonel Greenaway commented.

'It looks very like it, Colonel. The first job is to delve into Redshaw's background and past history, and that's the sort of thing the Yard's geared to. I've already rung my AC's office and asked them to get cracking on it. We'll hand over all the hiker's stuff to the forensic department as soon as we get up there tonight. Meanwhile, can you handle some of the local enquiries at this end? How did the fellow get to North Pyrford, for instance?'

'Can do, can't we Canning? We'll contact all neighbouring forces. You might let us have a copy of the P-M report for any of the chap's physical characteristics.'

'Then there's the question of Redshaw's movements on June the eleventh last year,' Pollard went on. 'Enquiries about those are going to be dicey, but it would be a start to know for sure that he was at home at the time.'

'What beats me is the chap's sheer nerve,' Inspector Frost said suddenly. 'Going off to the States as large as life the very morning after your broadcast, Mr Pollard.'

'A certain amount of calculation there, don't you think? No doubt he'd talked a lot about this dinner, and to cry off suddenly would have surprised people locally. And it suggests that he's completely confident that the link between the hiker and himself can never be traced. Well, we've got to prove him wrong, that's all.'

'There's this problem of Aldridge,' Colonel Greenaway

156

said. 'I think you're right about his being at risk if Redshaw turns up and finds that this stolen goods business has come out, and Aldridge could mention seeing him pass the quarry. Difficult to know what to do. Aldridge is sure to get bail when he comes up before the Bench, and we can't stop him going home.'

'May I come in here, sir?' Frost asked. 'I've been over to see his wife, and it's a rum set up. All that I could get out of her was that she knew nothing whatever about the shop bar the Post Office work, and that she shouldn't think he'd want to show his face in Pyrford again.'

'It sounds as though she's known all along what he's been up to, and been scared stiff and had enough. Well, we can only wait and see what he does. You said you'd asked the Yard to contact the FBI, didn't you, Pollard? Let us know if the Redshaws suddenly head for home ... I expect you want to be off, don't you, if you're calling in on Bosworth at Marchester before you get your train?'

There was little time to spare, and Toye did the run to Marchester at an exhilarating speed. As always, being in action raised Pollard's spirits. At any rate, he thought, watching the headlights rip up the darkness, we're on the right track at long last, whatever we run up against.

Superintendent Bosworth, chagrined by his men's failure to trace George Aldridge's departure from the city on 19 November, was initially a little distant. He thawed, however, on being given a full account of developments up to date and getting a further request for help. He jotted down Hugh Redshaw's alleged movements on leaving the Consistory Court, and shook his head.

'Pack of lies,' he said. 'It may take a bit of time to clear up, seeing we'll have to use indirect methods, but I've got a chap who's a real dab at getting information out of people without their noticing. We'll keep in touch by phone. Your number and extension? Thanks, Inspector ... Run you to the station, shall we?'

Ten minutes later the London train began to pull out.

'Quite a day,' Pollard remarked, settling in a corner of an empty compartment. 'Let's close down *pro tem* and get some sleep.'

A few minutes later he looked across to see Toye already neatly and composedly sleeping, but his own mind remained obstinately active. From long experience he knew that the only thing to do on these occasions was to let one's thoughts drift. He found himself as it were standing back, and viewing the case with objective interest. It had presented odd features from the start, being a curious blend of the commonplace and the fantastic: a crude brutal assault on an elderly woman interwoven with an almost incredible story of a missing chalice of great value. Not directly involved in the enquiry, but constantly looming in the background, was the figure of that aged eccentric, Barnabas Viney, whose striking face rose up vividly in Pollard's memory. The whole business of the chalice had been a waste of time, but worth it, he told himself defiantly, remembering the moment in the sunshine in Ambercombe churchyard when he had first held the precious thing in his hands. Not the reaction of a responsible CID Super, perhaps, but that was how one felt ... There had followed a sequence of unexpected events: Rosemary Gillard's attempted suicide, the discovery of the body in the quarry pool, George Aldridge's unconscious revelation that Hugh Redshaw had returned to Pyrford early enough on the afternoon of 19 November to murder Ethel Ridd, and finally the fortuitous discovery of the way in which he could have concealed the real time of his return ... all ... through ... that ... damn ... bus ... moving ... out ...

As the train eventually reached the approaches to Paddington, rushing over one set of points after another, Pollard stood in his dream on a seashore, watching the breakers coming in in rapid succession, sweeping white fragments of foam towards him. In his distress at being unable to grasp any of these he woke to see Toye bringing their suitcases down from the rack. He gave an immense yawn and stretched.

'So what?' he said. 'We'll call in at the Yard, get the machinery switched on, and make for home.'

By half past nine on the following morning he was back at

158

his desk, preparatory to embarking upon the stage in a case which he heartily disliked.

'I can't take this business of being a sort of ruddy computer,' he complained to Toye. 'Sitting here on my bottom and being programmed with data I can't verify myself, and being expected to spit out the right answer at the end of it. And you needn't go all reasonable and start pointing out that we couldn't cover the ground ourselves in the time.'

Toye grinned and enquired about the report from the ballistics experts which had just come in.

'I'll admit that it's more definite than we expected. They say it's a 70:30 likelihood that the bullet was fired by the Colt ·38. Quite a useful straw in the wind, in fact. We'd better start on an interim report for the AC now, and then fill in time clearing up arrears while we're hanging about.'

Further items of information came in at intervals as the hours passed. The shoes retrieved from the quarry pool were identified as a make popular with the outdoor man in the States. Starting from the date of Hugh Redshaw's birth given as 1922 in *Who's Who*, a searcher located his birth certificate. He had been born at Mitcham, son of Leonard Redshaw, grocer, and his wife Ena. Enquiries were proceeding at Mitcham. Superintendent Bosworth reported from Marchester that Hugh Redshaw's suggested witness of his alleged arrival in the bar of the Cathedral Hotel had turned out to be an old dodderer, adding that either side could make mincemeat of him in court, if it came to that. Enquiries at the public library were proceeding. Then, after a static early afternoon, there was a sudden invitation to go along to the forensic laboratory which was dealing with the scrap of paper discovered by Toye in the thicket above the old quarry at Ambercombe. Responding with alacrity, they found one of the senior scientists and a couple of young technicians clustered round a brightly lit area on a bench, and were greeted with the usual contumely.

'All right, all right,' Pollard retorted. 'We'll take it as read, Blake, that it was an impossible job which only the brilliance and tenacity of you and your minions could have pulled off. What – if anything of the slightest use – have you managed to bring up?'

'Look for yourselves,' Richard Blake, a friend of long standing replied. 'If you can understand a blown-up photograph, that is.'

The magnified paper appeared to consist of large chunks of straw and other substances which mysteriously held together.

The page number 44 stood out clearly. Faintly discernible but legible were the opening words of four lines of print.

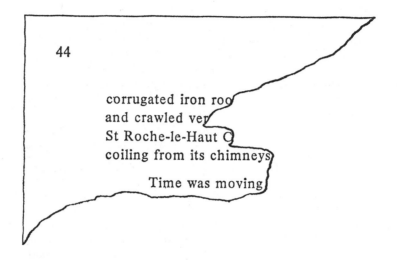

44

corrugated iron roo
and crawled ver
St Roche-le-Haut C
coiling from its chimneys
Time was moving

As Pollard stared at the photograph he became aware of suppressed hilarity.

'Got it?' enquired the scientist.

'Got what?'

'Don't you ever open a book, man? It's a bit of Redshaw's *Backdrop*, that Resistance thriller that sent him up to the top of the charts. We spotted the name of the place: St Roche-le-Haut-Clocher, and sent out for a copy. Here, have a look.'

Pollard took the paperback handed to him, open at page 44, and read:

corrugated iron roof of the hut. Emerging on hands and knees he kept low and crawled very cautiously to the

gap. Below lay St Roche-le-Haut Clocher apparently deserted but with smoke coiling from its chimneys.
Time was moving fast, and action of some sort was ...

'As it happens,' he said, returning the paperback, 'you chaps have stumbled on something by sheer accident that could be quite useful. Glad we were able to find a job to keep you occupied.'

During the next forty-eight hours information continued to trickle in slowly, the most important item being the news that the Redshaw family had moved from Mitcham to the holiday resort of Whitecliffe Bay on the south coast in 1924.

'Not so good,' Pollard commented. 'It's a place that's grown enormously, with a big influx of population. There must have been a lot of redevelopment. If Redshaw *père* opened a shop there in 1924, it's probably been demolished by now. They won't be easy to trace.'

More encouragingly a jubilant Superintendent Bosworth rang from Marchester to say that they had bust Hugh Redshaw's alibi at the public library wide open. No one was prepared to swear to the exact time of his arrival, but there was agreement that it was during the lunch hour, and well before two o'clock. As a local celebrity he was accorded certain privileges, among them that of taking reference books to a small room on the first floor used for storage, so that he could work undisturbed. It had a door on to an outside escape, and questioning had brought to light the fact that a cleaner had found this unbolted a couple of days later. She had not reported it, being afraid that she had forgotten to shoot the bolt herself on her last visit, when she had opened the fire escape door to shake out her duster. It had also been noticed that the books Hugh Redshaw had asked for had not been brought back to the main library, but left in the room, a departure from his usual practice.

'Useful,' Toye said, incorporating this report into the file.

Pollard, who was beginning to feel the nervous strain of waiting and continued inaction, gave an assenting grunt. At the back of his mind was a teasing suspicion that even now some unpredictable development would mean altering the whole course of the enquiry.

161

The first real breakthrough came just as they returned from lunch. Investigations at Whitecliffe Bay had unearthed a reliable source of information about the Redshaw family. Both the CID sergeant working in Whitecliffe and the local police felt that it would be worthwhile for Mr Pollard to come down.

'We'll go by train,' Pollard said, buzzing his secretary. 'There's a good service, and it'll be quicker than by road.'

The reliable source of information proved to be the Reverend John Morley, formerly vicar of St Faith's, the old parish church of Whitecliffe Bay, now a widower, and living in a bungalow provided by the diocesan authorities for their retired clergy.

'If he's another Barnabas Viney, I'll be sending in my resignation,' Pollard remarked, as they rang the bell and waited on the doorstep of the little bungalow.

Any apprehensions of this kind were quickly dispelled by an alert glance from the small whitehaired figure who opened the door and greeted them.

'That nice fellow Inspector Pye came to say that you'd be calling,' the old man said. 'Come inside. It's a bit small, but very snug.'

The little sitting room into which they were ushered had a masculine cosiness, with well-filled bookcases, shabby but comfortable chairs, and photographs of groups of various types of humanity on the walls. A tabby cat asleep in front of a gas fire raised its head to give the callers a critical glance, and returned to its slumbers.

'I suggest a cup of tea and a Garibaldi biscuit,' Mr Morley said. 'I always have one about now, and I don't mind saying that I make a very good cup of tea. In fact, I've become quite handy in the kitchen since I lost my dear wife two years ago.'

'A cup of tea's just what we're feeling like,' Pollard said, 'and I haven't had a Garibaldi biscuit for years, have you, Toye?'

The tea was quickly forthcoming, and was hot and good.

'Now, I wonder why you've come to me about the Redshaws,' Mr Morley said, giving his visitors a shrewd glance.

'You'd have had no difficulty in finding Hugh, now that he's so well-known. Surely it can't be poor Douglas after all these years?'

Pollard felt a sudden stillness go through him.

'Douglas, sir?' he asked.

'Yes, yes. The adopted son. Perhaps they were a little precipitate in adopting a child, but they were terribly disappointed at not having a family of their own, and the doctors said they couldn't hold out any hope. Then Hugh came along, you see, a couple of years later. It was almost bound to cause difficulties as the boys grew up.'

A clear picture of the Redshaw *ménage* emerged with the help of an occasional question from Pollard. John Morley had come to Whitecliffe Bay in 1935 as Rector of St Faith's, and found the family among the regular members of his congregation. By that time Leonard Redshaw had built up a thriving grocery business, and both boys were at the local grammar school.

'It was a good sound home,' John Morley pursued. 'An educated one, up to a certain standard, with books in it, and Mrs Redshaw was a splendid manager. The only trouble was the tension between Douglas and Hugh. You see, Hugh resented Douglas – there'd never been any secret about the adoption – and always wanted to go one better, although he was two years younger. I mean, if Douglas got into a team, Hugh was like a bear with a sore head until he won a cup for something, and so on. It was the same over their school work. Naturally Douglas went all out to keep ahead, but as he moved into his adolescent stage he began to react differently, and gave the parents a lot of worry. He was difficult at home, and took up with not very desirable boys, and girls too, I'm afraid. His work went off, and he left school at sixteen and started drifting in and out of jobs. Meanwhile Hugh left with a good School Certificate and went into one of the local banks. Then, of course, the war came, and they were both called up . . . Do let me give you second cups.'

Both boys came through the war. Hugh returned to the bank, but Douglas left home, saying he'd found a job in London. He kept more or less in touch, but the Redshaws could not find out exactly what he was doing, and were

163

worried about him. Finally he got into bad company, and was wanted by the police in connection with robbery with violence in a London suburb, in the course of which an elderly man was coshed and killed. He contrived to give them the slip, and had never been traced.

'It was a most terrible business for the Redshaws,' John Morley went on. 'They were such a respectable family, and you can imagine the talk. Whitecliffe was a much smaller place then, and everybody knew everybody else's affairs. And Leonard and Ena Redshaw were genuinely fond of Douglas, with all his failings. So was I. In fact I liked him a lot better than Hugh, who was always so preoccupied with getting on. And so he has, of course. I believe he started writing as a sideline, and did so well that he was able to give up a career in banking and become a full-time author.'

Both Redshaw parents had died in the nineteen-fifties, leaving the grocery business to Hugh, who by this time had a post in a London branch of his bank. He had sold the shop premises and goodwill, and disappeared from the Whitecliffe scene. There had been several subsequent changes of owner-ship, and recently a supermarket chain had bought out the current proprietor, as well as several of his neighbours, in order to demolish a sufficient number of buildings to re-develop extensively and open on a large scale in White-cliffe.

Pollard sat thoughtfully drinking a third cup of tea as John Morley filled in these details.

'What did Douglas Redshaw look like, sir?' he asked presently.

For the first time the old priest was slightly at a loss. There had been nothing very special about the lad's ap-pearance, he said. Perhaps a bit below average height. Not a hefty chap, but wiry. Good at games and handy with a boat. The usual sort of brown hair.

'It's all a long time ago, and my memory isn't what it was,' he said apologetically, 'especially for faces. Of course, it's fifteen years since I retired, and I'm getting on. I'm afraid I haven't been a great deal of help, and I can't think of anyone who's likely to remember the Redshaws any better. People move about so much these days.'

164

Pollard assured him that he had been a great deal of help, but it was clear that this source of information had run dry, and after a short interval said that it was time he and Toye made for their train back to London.

'If this Douglas Redshaw was the hiker,' Toye said as they walked away, 'how do you suppose he got to the States, as seems likely from his accent and the shoes?'

'No real difficulty there, I should think, at that particular time. There must have been quite a brisk traffic in passports just after the war. My guess is that he bought a Yank one and got it duly tarted up. He was in with the criminal class.'

'What brought him back after all these years, do you suppose?'

'This is the question, isn't it? Perhaps he came on one of Hugh's books over there, and realised from the jacket blurb that his brother by adoption was making a packet from film rights and whatever. He can hardly have expected a handout from all accounts, so it does look as though a spot of blackmail was the idea.'

'Fits in with the way they met up,' Toye agreed. 'In the middle of nowhere, you might say, instead of Douglas going to the house. Jacket blurbs often say more or less where a writer lives, don't they? I reckon the meeting place was fixed up by that telephone call from North Pyrford.'

'The odd thing is, though,' Pollard said, 'that instead of Douglas Redshaw being in a position to blackmail Hugh, it looks as though the boot was on the other leg. After all, Douglas was a fugitive from justice, in connection with armed robbery and a homicide. Whereas Hugh, on the face of it, has had a blameless life as a bank official and writer of improbable whodunits. In other words, this unspeakable case is standing on its head yet again. Always assuming the hiker *was* Douglas Redshaw, as you say.'

The following days were devoted to a follow-up of the information gathered at Whitecliffe Bay. Toye investigated police records of the robbery and homicide in which Douglas Redshaw had been involved, including the subsequent histories of his two associates who had been arrested and ultimately sentenced. In spite of all efforts Douglas Redshaw had managed to slip through the net and vanish without trace. In the opinion of the police he had provided the necessary brain power for the crime, and had cleared off leaving the other two to carry the can in complete ignorance of his escape route. The United States immigration authorities had no record of anyone of the name of Douglas Redshaw entering the country by the official channels, and similar information came through from Canada. Further co-operation was promised, but it was pointed out, in the Yard's view unnecessarily, that there was very little to go on.

In the meantime Pollard concentrated on Hugh Redshaw's past with the aim of uncovering any activities lending themselves to blackmail at a later date. In this he met with no success whatever. The bank which had employed him produced a record of efficient reliable service, and added that his resignation had been received with regret. The landlady in whose house he had lodged on first coming to London was traced, and also the proprietress of a private hotel in Kensington to which he had subsequently moved. Nothing to his discredit emerged beyond the opinion that he was a selfish type and keener on Number One than anything else. Approaching Thrale's, Hugh Redshaw's publishers, clearly presented difficulties. Pollard finally decided to send along a promising young CID sergeant with literary tastes in the guise of a freelance writer, working on a study of crime fiction in the post-war period. His modest request to check up on the publication dates of Hugh Redshaw's early books led on to some friendly chat about the author, one of Thrale's top sellers. However, little that was new emerged beyond the fact that he had married into the money all right. Miranda Redshaw was pretty well-heeled in her own right, and her sob-stuff verses brought in a packet, believe it or not. Of course, Thrale's didn't handle that sort of thing ...

Finally, with the not unfamiliar feeling of being up against a brick wall, Pollard compiled a detailed report for his Assistant Commissioner, setting out the case against Hugh Redshaw as far as it could be taken on the evidence available.

'That's that,' he remarked to Toye, after reading through

the pages of typescript and signing the last one with a defiant flourish. 'What's the betting that we're called off within the next day or two?'

All that remained seemed to be to cultivate a philosophical attitude, and when summoned to the Assistant Commissioner's office a couple of days later, he went along more or less reconciled to an inevitable shelving of the case.

'I've spent quite a bit of time on this,' the AC told him, indicating the report lying on his desk. 'One of your disproportionately large number of interesting cases, Pollard, even if the answer looks like being a lemon. There's one factual error in your report, by the way.'

'Sir?' Nettled, Pollard hastily searched his memory.

'Yes. You say Hugh Redshaw's first book, *Deadly Venom*, came out in 1958. Actually it was first published in '48, under a pen name and different title. I picked up a copy on a secondhand book stall some years ago, and recognised the plot at once.'

Pollard had a sudden sense of groping in the dark, together with astonishment at the AC's literary taste.

'I'm surprised that you read whodunits, sir,' he said feebly.

'Indeed?' To Pollard's further astonishment an impish expression flickered briefly across the normally impassive official countenance. 'I've a collection of well over a thousand at home. When I retire I'm going to write a book on crime fiction. Not one of these encyclopedic affairs, but a devastating study of popular fictional detectives. God knows I've suffered enough from the genuine article.'

'Sir,' Pollard broke in, hardly listening, 'who published that '48 edition?'

The AC rummaged in his brief case and extracted a faded tatty paperback.

'Trumpet Books. *Cobra Coils* by Murgatroyd Mitcham,' he said. 'It could hardly have been on worse paper or more badly printed. Still, there were shortages of everything for a long time after the war.'

'I'm certain from what we got from Thrale's that they

didn't know about this early edition of – what is it – *Deadly Venom*?' Pollard told him.

'What are you driving at, for heaven's sake? That the hiker was the chap who ran Trumpet Books, and who had just cottoned on to the reissue by Thrales seventeen years ago, and turned up in fancy dress to demand royalties with menaces?'

Illumination came with such suddenness that Pollard was speechless for a moment.

'Suppose Hugh Redshaw never wrote the book at all – or only tarted it up? Suppose Douglas Redshaw wrote it, and had to fade out before it was published because of the robbery? If he's been in the States all this time and not doing particularly well from the look of it, he might quite easily only just have discovered that Hugh had pinched his book.'

There was a lengthy pause.

'One advantage of my extensive reading of crime novels which you clearly despise,' the AC said, 'is that I've become both critical and discriminating in this particular sphere. A Redshaw plot has an easily recognisable hallmark. I think we'd better take steps to find out what happened to Trumpet Books. I'll get on to old Hatherleigh. He's retired now, but the old boy was a leading literary agent for about fifty years, and he's got an elephant's memory. No time like the present. I'll ring him now. Listen in on the extension if you like.'

As Pollard hastened to do so, he wondered if he had ever eavesdropped a conversation more avidly. Mr Hatherleigh answered the telephone in person, and after pleasantries and some personal chat, the AC applied a touch of flattery and enquired about Trumpet Books.

'Trumpet Books ... Trumpet Books,' a rasping elderly voice repeated. 'Wait a bit. Don't hustle the old fellow ... I'll get it in a moment.'

There was an apparently endless interval of silence during which Pollard realised that he was rigid with tension. He furtively stretched his cramped legs.

'It was one of those post-war mushroom stunts,' Mr Hatherleigh suddenly announced without preamble. 'Crackpot young chap out of the forces put his gratuity into a small printing works, and thought he'd have a go at bringing out

168

paperbacks. We never sent him anything, but if you've got a Trumpet Book he must have contacted its author somehow. Somebody who'd never been in print before, I expect.'

'Did the business just fold?' the AC asked.

'The place burnt down one night, and the chap – Harcourt, his name was, I remember – collected the insurance money and faded out. Funny you should ask me about him. I came across an article in a magazine at the Club the other day. He seems to have taken up thatching and be doing very well in the Midlands somewhere.'

'*Thatching?*'

'Yes. People don't stick to their last these days, do they? Perhaps that's why there's so much shoddy work about ... Well, glad I could help Scotland Yard. When are you going to look me up again?'

Several minutes later the AC put down the receiver and turned to Pollard.

'I imagine,' he said, 'that it won't be too difficult for you to track down a thatcher in the Midlands called Harcourt, who's doing well enough to feature in a magazine article.'

Mr Harcourt was located in a matter of hours. At mid-morning of the following day Pollard and Toye arrived in a Warwickshire village by a slow-flowing river in a setting of prosperous farmland and fine trees. They were directed to a timber and brick house on the outskirts, elegantly thatched and flanked by a large yard. The doors of the latter stood open and they walked in. Stacks of reeds were covered with tarpaulins. Bales of twine were stacked under lean-to roofs. There were innumerable ladders, a muddy Land Rover and an estate car. Down one side of the yard was a display window for baskets, wicker chairs and similar goods. There was no sign of life.

'Anyone around?' Pollard called.

A tall man, in ancient trousers and a tweed jacket with elbows reinforced with leather patches, appeared in the doorway of a shed and came towards them. He was bald on the top with an encircling fringe of greying hair, ruddy-complexioned, and had a turned-up nose and a buoyant expression.

169

'If you want your roof done, gentlemen,' he said, 'we're completely booked until next autumn.'

'Unfortunately neither of us has that sort of roof,' Pollard told him. 'Are you Mr Harcourt?'

'I am Tim Harcourt. What can I do for you?'

'Give us ten minutes or so of your time, if you'll be so good,' Pollard replied, holding out his official card.

Tim Harcourt inspected it and gave a shout of laughter.

'Can it be that the sins of my youth have caught up on me? Come into the office and break it gently.'

The office was small and rather untidy. There were two upright chairs, and Mr Harcourt propped himself against a filing cabinet. He listened with obvious astonishment as Pollard stated the purpose of the visit.

'Trumpet Books? Good Lord, that was another life. I was damn glad to get out of it all, to be honest. I was nuts to buy the works, but when you've been in a war you find you've lost your eye for a bit when you come out. But it wasn't arson. The insurance company were satisfied, and I met all my commitments like a perfect little gent.'

'I simply must ask you unofficially what made you switch from printing and tentative publishing to thatching,' Pollard said, unable to contain his curiosity any longer.

'It came out of a hat, actually. I mean, I was at a loose end and had the insurance money, so I thought of all the sort of jobs that had ever appealed to me, wrote 'em on bits of paper, and pulled one out of a hat. I've never regretted it for a moment. I learnt the trade, and bought this business. My wife's developed the basket-work side,' he added, with a wave in the direction of the display window, 'and both our boys have come in with me. We just can't meet the demand, that's the only trouble, apart from rising costs.'

'Quite a story,' Pollard commented rather enviously while conscious of waves of disapproval radiating from Toye. 'To get back to business, what we've chiefly come to see you about is a paperback you published back in '48, called *Cobra Coils*.'

'Good God, you don't mean that rum bloke calling himself Murgatroyd Mitcham's turned up?' Tim Harcourt exclaimed. 'I did everything I could to contact him after prac-

170

tically every copy of *Cobra Coils* went up in the fire, but he'd vanished without trace. He never would give me an address: just blew in when he felt like it.'

By dint of questioning Pollard elicited the facts of the business relationship between the two men. They had met in a bar at the time when Tim Harcourt was contemplating his Trumpet Books project. Mitcham had been interested, saying that he had filled in boring spells of inactivity in the army by working out plots for sensational thrillers, one of which, *Cobra Coils*, he had written up. Tim Harcourt had read it, decided that it had possibilities, and offered a small advance and a royalties scale had been agreed on.

'Did you see any of the other plots?' Pollard asked.

'No. He said he'd left them in his people's place down in Southshire, and would collect them next time he went home ... Look here, just what is all this in aid of? Chaps of your rank hunt bigger game, surely? Why doesn't Mitcham employ a lawyer if he thinks I'm sitting on cash he's entitled to?'

'I can see that you've no idea that you yourself are being done out of cash you're entitled to,' Pollard replied. 'You see, somebody else got hold of an odd copy of *Cobra Coils*, sat on it for some time, and then published it as his own effort.'

'The hell he did! Just lead me to him! Is Mitcham gunning for him too?'

'To the best of our knowledge and belief we got Mitcham out of a pool in a quarry recently, with a bag of stones round his neck and a bullet in his head.'

'Good Lord!' Tim Harcourt looked appalled. 'Any idea whodunit?'

'Yes. A definite idea but no conclusive proof. The man who pirated *Cobra Coils*. That's where we may want your help.'

'Well, of course, I'm on. What do you want me to do?'

'It's possible we may ask you to come along to this chap and start being aggressive about the book being pinched. There would be an element of risk, of course.'

'Fine. I can look after myself all right. Not to worry.'

'That's exactly what you might not do, Mr Harcourt,'

Pollard told him emphatically. 'Your personal safety would obviously be the responsibility of the police.'

'OK,' Tim Harcourt said regretfully. 'I take your point. When and where?'

'If you're needed, you'll be contacted by telephone. By the way, what did Mitcham look like?'

'Quite a bit shorter than me. Say five foot eight. Not a hefty type, but tough. Brown hair. I can't remember the colour of his eyes.'

After impressing the need for absolute discretion about their visit on Tim Harcourt, Pollard left with Toye to return to the Yard. As he expected, Toye was dubious about the confrontation idea.

'Redshaw's killed two people already,' he said.

'I know, and unless we're damn careful my guess is that Aldridge will be the third. But let's face it. We keep on collecting useful bits of evidence, but they're all highly circumstantial. Unless we can link Hugh Redshaw conclusively with Douglas, a case against him simply wouldn't stand up. Anyway, I'm putting the confrontation scheme to the AC.'

The train journey back to London gave Pollard an interval for further thought, and on arriving at the Yard he rang Robert Hoyle to ask if there were any news of the Redshaws' return from New York.

'I'm so glad you've rung,' Robert Hoyle said. 'I've been wondering if I ought to get on to you through Westbridge. They're due back the day after tomorrow, sometime in the afternoon. They're driving down from Heathrow.'

Pollard thanked him, and said that he and Toye might turn up tomorrow.

'How's the Aldridge situation developing?' he asked.

'He's out on bail, and living in a room in Westbridge apparently. He has to report to the police each day. He's refused to see me. Meanwhile, Mrs Aldridge is running the shop and getting a lot of local backing. She's a different creature. I've no idea what the final outcome will be. Frost says he – Aldridge – is seeing a lot of his solicitor. I suppose he could be making over the business to his wife preparatory to clearing out if he isn't jailed. By the way, there's one bit of good news, largely owing to you. Money's pouring in for the Ambercombe Church Restoration Fund. It was finding the chalice did it. The pundits seem quite sure it is the Tadenham Abbey one.'

Pollard congratulated Robert Hoyle, rang off, and went to keep his appointment with his Assistant Commissioner, who reacted with unconcealed satisfaction to the news that Murgatroyd Mitcham, alias Douglas Redshaw, had constructed other plots for thrillers.

'I was absolutely certain that all Hugh Redshaw's came from the same stable,' he said. 'This scheme of yours wants very careful consideration, though, Pollard. Think of the public reaction if he whips out another Colt and kills this Harcourt fellow. Or you and Toye. He's bound to have heard about the finding of the body and be dangerously on edge. Can you rely on Harcourt?'

After prolonged discussion Pollard was authorised to go ahead, with certain provisos. A third CID officer was to go too, purporting to be Tim Harcourt's solicitor. All three detectives were to be armed.

There was a good deal to arrange in the course of the next twenty-four hours, including the briefing of Tim Harcourt by telephone, and introducing Detective-Sergeant Mountsey, an ex-Commando selected as their support, to the intricacies of the situation. Pollard firmly declined, however, to make a detailed plan of action, pointing out that it would be a sheer waste of time.

'We don't even know who'll come to the front door,' he argued. 'I agree that you and Harcourt follow on at a two-minute interval – unless you hear shots, that is, and make it at the double. Four of us in a row would be enough to make any shady type pull out a gun. But beyond that we'll have to play it by ear.'

He did not give as an additional reason for flexibility the possibility of yet another unpredictable development in the case, even at the eleventh hour, confounding all expectations.

The Yard party left by road to spend the night before the Redshaws' return at Westbridge. This involved a tedious morning of waiting about, which Pollard felt was preferable to risking a delay *en route*, and a late arrival the next day. They held an informal conference with the Westbridge authorities, learnt that George Aldridge was still showing no inclination to leave the town, and waited interminably for a cruising Panda car to report the Redshaws' arrival at Pyrford. This message came through soon after two o'clock.

Half an hour later the party of four left in two cars. At Pyrford Sergeant Mountsey and Tim Harcourt parked on the Green, while Pollard and Toye drove up to the Old Rectory.

'Into battle,' Pollard remarked, and rang the bell.

Miranda Redshaw opened it, looking at them in vague surprise as recognition dawned only slowly in her wide-opened eyes. Pollard was apologetic. He knew they had only just arrived, but would it be possible to have just a word with Mr Redshaw? To his relief she smiled at him sweetly, and made no difficulty. Normally her husband would have been writing, of course, but as they were only just back he was only opening his tiresome mail ... What terrible ugly things had been happening in lovely Pyrford ...

So they know about the body, Pollard thought, as they crossed the hall. Miranda Redshaw opened the study door. 'Superintendent Pollard, Hugh dear,' she announced. 'He won't keep you a moment.'

A desk littered with envelopes and packages. The open door of an unsuspected wall safe. A quick tense glance from the man at the desk, succeeded by slightly cagey small talk about New York. Voices announcing the arrival of Mountsey and Harcourt at the front door. An interminable delay calling for a nerve-wracking effort to keep the conversation going. At last Miranda Redshaw was at the door again.

'Two gentlemen Superintendent Pollard asked to join him here,' she said.

Pollard saw the danger signal: a curious reddening of Hugh Redshaw's eyes like those of a threatened animal. He also saw Toye and Mountsey achieving unobtrusive out-flanking movements, one on each side of the desk.

'Good afternoon,' Tim Harcourt said uncompromisingly. 'I've come to discuss your profits on *Deadly Venom*, alias

Cobra Coils, Redshaw. I happen to have published *Cobra Coils.*'

A number of events were so swiftly consecutive as to appear simultaneous. Toye seized Hugh Redshaw's hand on its way to his mouth. A window pane splintered. There was a loud report, and the man at the desk slumped forward. A second report came from the direction of the terrace, followed by a thud.

'Keep his wife out,' Pollard shouted, dashing across the room.

He flung up the window and looked down at George Aldridge, face downwards on the terrace, an automatic still clutched in his hand, and a tiny trickle of blood appearing on the gravel.

The final twist, he thought . . .

'Here you are,' the Assistant Commissioner said, passing over an untidy bundle of scribbled notes. 'I've equated every one of these outlined plots with one of Hugh Redshaw's books. The critics always said his plots were better than his characterisation and writing. There are three he hasn't used, by the way. God only knows what the legal position is in all this . . . You know, I've quite enjoyed being what you might call actively involved in a case again.'

Pollard made the obviously called-for remark to the effect that the involvement had led to the solution.

'Not entirely. You did a bit of preliminary work, I'll grant you that. It's important to be able to delegate though, particularly as a Detective-Chief-Superintendent. That's all just for the moment, I think, Pollard.'

Pollard contrived to look suitably deadpan. 'Thank you, sir,' he said.